Juana

Honore de Balzac

Contents

JUANA

BY

Honore de Balzac

CHAPTER I
EXPOSITION

Notwithstanding the discipline which Marechal Suchet had introduced into his army corps, he was unable to prevent a short period of trouble and disorder at the taking of Tarragona. According to certain fair-minded military men, this intoxication of victory bore a striking resemblance to pillage, though the marechal promptly suppressed it. Order being re-established, each regiment quartered in its respective lines, and the commandant of the city appointed, military administration began. The place assumed a mongrel aspect. Though all things were organized on a French system, the Spaniards were left free to follow "in petto" their national tastes.

This period of pillage (it is difficult to determine how long it lasted) had, like all other sublunary effects, a cause, not so difficult to discover. In the marechal's army was a regiment, composed almost entirely of Italians and commanded by a certain Colonel Eugene, a man of remarkable bravery, a second Murat, who, having entered the military service too late, obtained neither a Grand Duchy of Berg nor a Kingdom of Naples, nor balls at the Pizzo. But if he won no crown he had ample opportunity to obtain wounds, and it was not surprising that he met with several. His regiment was composed of the scattered fragments of the

Italian legion. This legion was to Italy what the colonial battalions are to France. Its permanent cantonments, established on the island of Elba, served as an honorable place of exile for the troublesome sons of good families and for those great men who have just missed greatness, whom society brands with a hot iron and designates by the term "mauvais sujets"; men who are for the most part misunderstood; whose existence may become either noble through the smile of a woman lifting them out of their rut, or shocking at the close of an orgy under the influence of some damnable reflection dropped by a drunken comrade.

Napoleon had incorporated these vigorous beings in the sixth of the line, hoping to metamorphose them finally into generals,--barring those whom the bullets might take off. But the emperor's calculation was scarcely fulfilled, except in the matter of the bullets. This regiment, often decimated but always the same in character, acquired a great reputation for valor in the field and for wickedness in private life. At the siege of Tarragona it lost its celebrated hero, Bianchi, the man who, during the campaign, had wagered that he would eat the heart of a Spanish sentinel, and did eat it. Though Bianchi was the prince of the devils incarnate to whom the regiment owed its dual reputation, he had, nevertheless, that sort of chivalrous honor which excuses, in the army, the worst excesses. In a word, he would have been, at an earlier period, an admirable pirate. A few days before his death he distinguished himself by a daring action which the marechal wished to reward. Bianchi refused rank, pension, and additional decoration, asking, for sole recompense, the favor of being the first to mount the breach at the assault on Tarragona. The marechal granted the request and then forgot his promise; but Bianchi forced him to remember Bianchi. The enraged hero was the first to plant our flag on the wall, where he was shot by a monk.

This historical digression was necessary, in order to explain how it was that the 6th of the line was the regiment to enter Tarragona, and why the disorder and confusion, natural enough in a city taken by storm, degenerated for a time into a slight pillage.

This regiment possessed two officers, not at all remarkable among these men of iron, who played, nevertheless, in the history we shall now relate, a somewhat important part.

The first, a captain in the quartermaster's department, an officer half civil, half military, was considered, in soldier phrase, to be fighting his own battle. He pretended bravery, boasted loudly of belonging to the 6th of the line, twirled his moustache with the air of a man who was ready to demolish everything; but his brother officers did not esteem him. The fortune he possessed made him cautious. He was nicknamed, for two reasons, "captain of crows." In the first place, he could smell powder a league off, and took wing at the sound of a musket; secondly, the nickname was based on an innocent military pun, which his position in the regiment warranted. Captain Montefiore, of the illustrious Montefiore family of Milan (though the laws of the Kingdom of Italy forbade him to bear his title in the French service) was one of the handsomest men in the army. This beauty may have been among the secret causes of his prudence on fighting days. A wound which might have injured his nose, cleft his forehead, or scarred his cheek, would have destroyed one of the most beautiful Italian faces which a woman ever dreamed of in all its delicate proportions. This face, not unlike the type which Girodet has given to the dying young Turk, in the "Revolt at Cairo," was instinct with that melancholy by which all women are more or less duped.

The Marquis de Montefiore possessed an entailed property, but his income was mortgaged for a number of years to pay off the costs of certain Italian escapades which are inconceivable in Paris. He had ruined himself in supporting a theatre at Milan in order to force upon a public a very inferior prima donna, whom he was said to love madly. A fine future was therefore before him, and he did not care to risk it for the paltry distinction of a bit of red ribbon. He was not a brave man, but he was certainly a philosopher; and he had precedents, if we may use so parliamentary an expression. Did not Philip the Second register a vow after the battle of Saint Quentin that never again would he put himself under fire? And did not the Duke of Alba encourage him in thinking that the worst trade in the world was the involuntary exchange of a crown for a bullet? Hence, Montefiore was Philippiste in his capacity of rich marquis and handsome man; and in other respects also he was quite as profound a politician as Philip the Second himself. He consoled himself for his nickname, and for the disesteem of the regiment by thinking that his comrades were blackguards, whose opinion would never be of any consequence to him if by chance they survived the present war, which seemed to be one of extermination. He relied on his face to win him promotion; he saw himself made colonel by feminine influence and a carefully managed transition from captain of equipment to orderly officer, and from orderly officer to aide-de-camp on the staff of some easy-going marshal. By that time, he reflected, he should come into his property of a hundred thousand scudi a year, some journal would speak of him as "the brave Montefiore," he would marry a girl of rank, and no one would dare to dispute his courage or verify his wounds.

Captain Montefiore had one friend in the person of the quartermaster, --a Provencal, born in the neighborhood of Nice, whose name was Diard. A friend, whether at the galleys or in the garret of an artist, consoles for many troubles. Now Montefiore and Diard were two philosophers, who consoled each other for their present lives by the study of vice, as artists soothe the immediate disappointment of their hopes by the expectation of future fame. Both regarded the war in its results, not its action; they simply considered those who died for glory fools. Chance had made soldiers of them; whereas their natural proclivities would have seated them at the green table of a congress. Nature had poured Montefiore into the mould of a Rizzio, and Diard into that of a diplomatist. Both were endowed with that nervous, feverish, half-feminine organization, which is equally strong for good or evil, and from which may emanate, according to the impulse of these singular temperaments, a crime or a generous action, a noble deed or a base one. The fate of such natures depends at any moment on the pressure, more or less powerful, produced on their nervous systems by violent and transitory passions.

Diard was considered a good accountant, but no soldier would have trusted him with his purse or his will, possibly because of the antipathy felt by all real soldiers against the bureaucrats. The quartermaster was not without courage and a certain juvenile generosity, sentiments which many men give up as they grow older, by dint of reasoning or calculating. Variable as the beauty of a fair woman, Diard was a great boaster and a great talker, talking of everything. He said he was artistic, and he made prizes (like two celebrated generals) of works of art, solely, he declared, to preserve them for posterity. His military comrades would have been puzzled indeed to form a correct judgment of him. Many of them, accustomed to draw upon his funds when occasion obliged them, thought him rich; but in truth, he was a gambler, and gamblers may be said to have nothing of their own. Montefiore was also a gambler, and all the officers of the regiment played with the pair; for, to the shame of men be it said, it is not a rare thing to see persons gambling together around a green table who, when the game is finished, will not bow to their companions, feeling no respect for them. Montefiore was the man with whom Bianchi made his bet about the heart of the Spanish senti-nel.

Montefiore and Diard were among the last to mount the breach at Tarragona, but the first in the heart of the town as soon as it was taken. Accidents of this sort happen in all attacks, but with this pair of friends they were customary. Supporting each other, they made their way bravely through a labyrinth of narrow and gloomy little streets in quest of their personal objects; one seeking for painted madonnas, the other for madonnas of flesh and blood.

In what part of Tarragona it happened I cannot say, but Diard pres-ently recognized by its architecture the portal of a convent, the gate of which was already battered in. Springing into the cloister to put a stop to the fury of the soldiers, he arrived just in time to prevent two Parisians from shooting a Virgin by Albano. In spite of the moustache with which in their military fanaticism they had decorated her face, he bought the picture. Montefiore, left alone during this episode, no-ticed, nearly opposite the convent, the house and shop of a draper, from which a shot was fired at him at the moment when his eyes caught a flaming glance from those of an inquisitive young girl, whose head was advanced under the shelter of a blind. Tarragona taken by assault, Tarragona furious, firing from every window, Tarragona violated, with dishevelled hair, and half-naked, was indeed an object of curiosity,--the curiosity of a daring Spanish woman. It was a magnified bull-fight.

Montefiore forgot the pillage, and heard, for the moment, neither the cries, nor the musketry, nor the growling of the artillery. The profile of that Spanish girl was the most divinely delicious thing which he, an Italian libertine, weary of Italian beauty, and dreaming of an impossible woman because he was tired of all women, had ever seen. He could still quiver, he, who had wasted his fortune on a thousand follies, the thousand passions of a young and blase man--the most abominable monster that society generates. An idea came into his head, suggested perhaps by the shot of the draper-patriot, namely,--to set fire to the house. But he was now alone, and without any means of action; the fighting was centred in the market-place, where a few obstinate beings were still defending the town. A better idea then occurred to him. Diard came out of the convent, but Montefiore said not a word of his discovery; on the contrary, he accompanied him on a series of rambles about the streets. But the next day, the Italian had obtained his military billet in the house of the draper,--an appropriate lodging for an equipment captain!

The house of the worthy Spaniard consisted, on the ground-floor, of a vast and gloomy shop, externally fortified with stout iron bars, such as we see in the old storehouses of the rue des Lombards. This shop communicated with a parlor lighted from an interior courtyard, a large room breathing the very spirit of the middle-ages, with smoky old pictures, old tapestries, antique "brazero," a plumed hat hanging to a nail, the musket of the guerrillas, and the cloak of Bartholo. The kitchen adjoined this unique living-room, where the inmates took their meals and warmed themselves over the dull glow of the brazier, smoking cigars and discoursing bitterly to animate all hearts with hatred against the French. Silver pitchers and precious dishes of plate and porcelain adorned a buttery shelf of the old fashion. But the light, sparsely admitted, allowed these dazzling objects to show but slightly; all things, as in pictures of the Dutch school, looked brown, even the faces. Between the shop and this living-room, so fine in color and in its tone of patriarchal life, was a dark staircase leading to a ware-room where the light, carefully distributed, permitted the examination of goods. Above this were the apartments of the merchant and his wife. Rooms for an apprentice and a servant-woman were in a garret under the roof, which projected over the street and was supported by buttresses, giving a somewhat fantastic appearance to the exterior of the building. These chambers were now taken by the merchant and his wife who gave up their own rooms to the officer who was billeted upon them,--probably because they wished to avoid all quarrelling.

Montefiore gave himself out as a former Spanish subject, persecuted by Napoleon, whom he was serving against his will; and these semi-lies had the success he expected. He was invited to share the meals of the family, and was treated with the respect due to his name, his birth, and his title. He had his reasons for capturing the good-will of the merchant and his wife; he scented his madonna as the ogre scented the youthful flesh of Tom Thumb and his brothers. But in spite of the confidence he managed to inspire in the worthy pair the latter maintained the most profound silence as to the said madonna; and not only did the captain see no trace of the young girl during the first day he spent under the roof of the honest Spaniard, but he heard no sound and came upon no indication which revealed her presence in that ancient building. Supposing that she was the only daughter of the old couple, Montefiore concluded they had consigned her to the garret, where, for the time being, they made their home.

But no revelation came to betray the hiding-place of that precious treasure. The marquis glued his face to the lozenge-shaped leaded panes which looked upon the black-walled enclosure of the inner courtyard; but in vain; he saw no gleam of light except from the windows of the old couple, whom he could see and hear as they went and came and talked and coughed. Of the young girl, not a shadow!

Montefiore was far too wary to risk the future of his passion by exploring the house nocturnally, or by tapping softly on the doors. Discovery by that hot patriot, the mercer, suspicious as a Spaniard must be, meant ruin infallibly. The captain therefore resolved to wait patiently, resting his faith on time and the imperfection of men, which always results--even with scoundrels, and how much more with honest men!--in the neglect of precautions.

The next day he discovered a hammock in the kitchen, showing plainly where the servant-woman slept. As for the apprentice, his bed was evidently made on the shop counter. During supper on the second day Montefiore succeeded, by cursing Napoleon, in smoothing the anxious forehead of the merchant, a grave, black-visaged Spaniard, much like the faces formerly carved on the handles of Moorish lutes; even the wife let a gay smile of hatred appear in the folds of her elderly face. The lamp and the reflections of the brazier illumined fantastically the shadows of the noble room. The mistress of the house offered a "cigarrito" to their semi-compatriot. At this moment the rustle of a dress and the fall of a chair behind the tapestry were plainly heard.

"Ah!" cried the wife, turning pale, "may the saints assist us! God grant no harm has happened!"

"You have some one in the next room, have you not?" said Montefiore, giving no sign of emotion.

The draper dropped a word of imprecation against the girls. Evidently alarmed, the wife opened a secret door, and led in, half fainting, the Italian's madonna, to whom he was careful to pay no attention; only, to avoid a too-studied indifference, he glanced at the girl before he turned to his host and said in his own language:--

"Is that your daughter, signore?"

Perez de Lagounia (such was the merchant's name) had large commercial relations with Genoa, Florence, and Livorno; he knew Italian, and replied in the same language:--

"No; if she were my daughter I should take less precautions. The child is confided to our care, and I would rather die than see any evil happen to her. But how is it possible to put sense into a girl of eighteen?"

"She is very handsome," said Montefiore, coldly, not looking at her face again.

"Her mother's beauty is celebrated," replied the merchant, briefly.

They continued to smoke, watching each other. Though Montefiore compelled himself not to give the slightest look which might contradict his apparent coldness, he could not refrain, at a moment when Perez turned his head to expectorate, from casting a rapid glance at the young girl, whose sparkling eyes met his. Then, with that science of vision which gives to a libertine, as it does to a sculptor, the fatal power of disrobing, if we may so express it, a woman, and divining her shape by inductions both rapid and sagacious, he beheld one of those masterpieces of Nature whose creation appears to demand as its right all the happiness of love. Here was a fair young face, on which the sun of Spain had cast faint tones of bistre which added to its expression of seraphic calmness a passionate pride, like a flash of light infused beneath that diaphanous complexion, --due, perhaps, to the Moorish blood which vivified and colored it. Her hair, raised to the top of her head, fell thence with black reflections round the delicate transparent ears and defined the outlines of a blue-veined throat. These luxuriant locks brought into strong relief the dazzling eyes and the scarlet lips of a well-arched mouth. The bodice of the country set off the lines of a figure that swayed as easily as a branch of willow. She was not the Virgin of Italy, but the Virgin of Spain, of Murillo, the only artist daring enough to have painted the Mother of God intoxicated with the joy of conceiving the Christ,--the glowing imagination of the boldest and also the warmest of painters.

In this young girl three things were united, a single one of which would have sufficed for the glory of a woman: the purity of the pearl in the depths of ocean; the sublime exaltation of the Spanish Saint Teresa; and a passion of love which was ignorant of itself. The presence of such a woman has the virtue of a talisman. Montefiore no longer felt worn and jaded. That young girl brought back his youthful freshness.

But, though the apparition was delightful, it did not last. The girl was taken back to the secret chamber, where the servant-woman carried to her openly both light and food.

"You do right to hide her," said Montefiore in Italian. "I will keep your secret. The devil! we have generals in our army who are capable of abducting her."

Montefiore's infatuation went so far as to suggest to him the idea of marrying her. He accordingly asked her history, and Perez very willingly told him the circumstances under which she had become his ward. The prudent Spaniard was led to make this confidence because he had heard of Montefiore in Italy, and knowing his reputation was desirous to let him see how strong were the barriers which protected the young girl from the possibility of seduction. Though the good-man was gifted with a certain patriarchal eloquence, in keeping with his simple life and customs, his tale will be improved by abridgment.

At the period when the French Revolution changed the manners and morals of every country which served as the scene of its wars, a street prostitute came to Tarragona, driven from Venice at the time of its fall. The life of this woman had been a tissue of romantic adventures and strange vicissitudes. To her, oftener than to any other woman of her class, it had happened, thanks to the caprice of great lords struck with her extraordinary beauty, to be literally gorged with gold and jewels and all the delights of excessive wealth, --flowers, carriages, pages, maids, palaces, pictures, journeys (like those of Catherine II.); in short, the life of a queen, despotic in her caprices and obeyed, often beyond her own imaginings. Then, without herself, or any one, chemist, physician, or man of science, being able to discover how her gold evaporated, she would find herself back in the streets, poor, denuded of everything, preserving nothing but her all-powerful beauty, yet living on without thought or care of the past, the present, or the future. Cast, in her poverty, into the hands of some poor gambling officer, she attached herself to him as a dog to its master, sharing the discomforts of the military life, which indeed she comforted, as content under the roof of a garret as beneath the silken hangings of opulence. Italian and Spanish both, she fulfilled very scrupulously the duties of religion, and more than once she had said to love:--

"Return to-morrow; to-day I belong to God."

But this slime permeated with gold and perfumes, this careless indifference to all things, these unbridled passions, these religious beliefs cast into that heart like diamonds into mire, this life begun, and ended, in a hospital, these gambling chances transferred to the soul, to the very existence,--in short, this great alchemy, for which vice lit the fire beneath the crucible in which fortunes were melted up and the gold of ancestors and the honor of great names evaporated, proceeded from a *cause*, a particular heredity, faithfully transmitted from mother to daughter since the middle ages. The name of this woman was La Marana. In her family, existing solely in the female line, the idea, person, name and power of a father had been completely unknown since the thirteenth century. The name Marana was to her what the designation of Stuart is to the celebrated royal race of Scotland, a name of distinction substituted for the patronymic name by the constant heredity of the same office devolving on the family.

Formerly, in France, Spain, and Italy, when those three countries had, in the fourteenth and fifteenth centuries, mutual interests which united and disunited them by perpetual warfare, the name Marana served to express in its general sense, a prostitute. In those days women of that sort had a certain rank in the world of which nothing in our day can give an idea. Ninon de l'Enclos and Marian Delorme have alone played, in France, the role of the Imperias, Catalinas, and Maranas who, in preceding centuries, gathered around them the cassock, gown, and sword. An Imperia built I forget which church in Rome in a frenzy of repentance, as Rhodope built, in earlier times, a pyramid in Egypt. The name Marana, inflicted at first as a disgrace upon the singular family with which we are now concerned, had ended by becoming its veritable name and by ennobling its vice by incontestable antiquity.

One day, a day of opulence or of penury I know not which, for this event was a secret between herself and God, but assuredly it was in a moment of repentance and melancholy, this Marana of the nineteenth century stood with her feet in the slime and her head raised to heaven. She cursed the blood in her veins, she cursed herself, she trembled lest she should have a daughter, and she swore, as such women swear, on the honor and with the will of the galleys--the firmest will, the most scrupulous honor that there is on earth--she swore, before an altar, and believing in that altar, to make her daughter a virtuous creature, a saint, and thus to gain, after that long line of lost women, criminals in love, an angel in heaven for them all.

The vow once made, the blood of the Maranas spoke; the courtesan returned to her reckless life, a thought the more within her heart. At last she loved, with the violent love of such women, as Henrietta Wilson loved Lord Ponsonby, as Mademoiselle Dupuis loved Bolingbroke, as the Marchesa Pescara loved her husband--but no, she did not love, she adored one of those fair men, half women, to whom she gave the virtues which she had not, striving to keep for herself all that there was of vice between them. It was from that weak man, that senseless marriage unblessed by God or man which happiness is thought to justify, but which no happiness absolves, and for which men blush at last, that she had a daughter, a daughter to save, a daughter for whom to desire a noble life and the chastity she had not. Henceforth, happy or not happy, opulent or beggared, she had in her heart a pure, untainted sentiment, the highest of all human feelings because the most disinterested. Love has its egotism, but motherhood has none. La Marana was a mother like none other; for, in her total, her eternal shipwreck, motherhood might still redeem her. To accomplish sacredly through life the task of sending a pure soul to heaven, was not that a better thing than a tardy repentance? was it not, in truth, the only spotless prayer which she could lift to God?

So, when this daughter, when her Marie-Juana-Pepita (she would fain have given her all the saints in the calendar as guardians), when this dear little creature was granted to her, she became possessed of so high an idea of the dignity of motherhood that she entreated vice to grant her a respite. She made herself virtuous and lived in solitude. No more fetes, no more orgies, no more love. All joys, all fortunes were centred now in the cradle of her child. The tones of that infant voice made an oasis for her soul in the burning sands of her existence. That sentiment could not be measured or estimated by any other. Did it not, in fact, comprise all human sentiments, all heavenly hopes? La Marana was so resolved not to soil her daughter with any stain other than that of birth, that she sought to invest her with social virtues; she even obliged the young father to settle a handsome patrimony upon the child and to give her his name. Thus the girl was not know as Juana Marana, but as Juana di Mancini.

Then, after seven years of joy, and kisses, and intoxicating happiness, the time came when the poor Marana deprived herself of her idol. That Juana might never bow her head under their hereditary shame, the mother had the courage to renounce her child for her child's sake, and to seek, not without horrible suffering, for another mother, another home, other principles to follow, other and saintlier examples to imitate. The abdication of a mother is either a revolting act or a sublime one; in this case, was it not sublime?

At Tarragona a lucky accident threw the Lagounias in her way, under circumstances which enabled her to recognize the integrity of the Spaniard and the noble virtue of his wife. She came to them at a time when her proposal seemed that of a liberating angel. The fortune and honor of the merchant, momentarily compromised, required a prompt and secret succor. La Marana made over to the husband the whole sum she had obtained of the father for Juana's "dot," requiring neither acknowledgment nor interest. According to her own code of honor, a contract, a trust, was a thing of the heart, and God its supreme judge. After stating the miseries of her position to Dona Lagounia, she confided her daughter and her daughter's fortune to the fine old Spanish honor, pure and spotless, which filled the precincts of that ancient house. Dona Lagounia had no child, and she was only too happy to obtain one to nurture. The mother then parted from her Juana, convinced that the child's future was safe, and certain of having found her a mother, a mother who would bring her up as a Mancini, and not as a Marana.

Leaving her child in the simple modest house of the merchant where the burgher virtues reigned, where religion and sacred sentiments and honor filled the air, the poor prostitute, the disinherited mother was enabled to bear her trial by visions of Juana, virgin, wife, and mother, a mother throughout her life. On the threshold of that house Marana left a tear such as the angels garner up.

Since that day of mourning and hope the mother, drawn by some invincible presentiment, had thrice returned to see her daughter. Once when Juana fell ill with a dangerous complaint:

"I knew it," she said to Perez when she reached the house.

Asleep, she had seen her Juana dying. She nursed her and watched her, until one morning, sure of the girl's convalescence, she kissed her, still asleep, on the forehead and left her without betraying whom she was. A second time the Marana came to the church where Juana made her first communion. Simply dressed, concealing herself behind a column, the exiled mother recognized herself in her daughter such as she once had been, pure as the snow fresh-fallen on the Alps. A courtesan even in maternity, the Marana felt in the depths of her soul a jealous sentiment, stronger for the moment than that of love, and she left the church, incapable of resisting any longer the desire to kill Dona Lagounia, as she sat there, with radiant face, too much the mother of her child. A third and last meeting had taken place between mother and daughter in the streets of Milan, to which city the merchant and his wife had paid a visit. The Marana drove through the Corso in all the splendor of a sovereign; she passed her daughter like a flash of lightning and was not recognized. Horrible anguish! To this Marana, surfeited with kisses, one was lacking, a single one, for which she would have bartered all the others: the joyous, girlish kiss of a daughter to a mother, an honored mother, a mother in whom shone all the domestic virtues. Juana living was dead to her. One thought revived the soul of the courtesan--a precious thought! Juana was henceforth safe. She might be the humblest of women, but at least she was not what her mother was--an infamous courtesan.

The merchant and his wife had fulfilled their trust with scrupulous integrity. Juana's fortune, managed by them, had increased tenfold. Perez de Lagounia, now the richest merchant in the provinces, felt for the young girl a sentiment that was semi-superstitious. Her money had preserved his ancient house from dishonorable ruin, and the presence of so precious a treasure had brought him untold prosperity. His wife, a heart of gold, and full of delicacy, had made the child religious, and as pure as she was beautiful. Juana might well become the wife of either a great seigneur or a wealthy merchant; she lacked no virtue necessary to the highest destiny. Perez had intended taking her to Madrid and marrying her to some grandee, but the events of the present war delayed the fulfilment of this project.

"I don't know where the Marana now is," said Perez, ending the above history, "but in whatever quarter of the world she may be living, when she hears of the occupation of our province by your armies, and of the siege of Tarragona, she will assuredly set out at once to come here and see to her daughter's safety."

CHAPTER II
AUCTION

The foregoing narrative changed the intentions of the Italian captain; no longer did he think of making a Marchesa di Montefiore of Juana di Mancini. He recognized the blood of the Maranas in the glance the girl had given from behind the blinds, in the trick she had just played to satisfy her curiosity, and also in the parting look she had cast upon him. The libertine wanted a virtuous woman for a wife.

The adventure was full of danger, but danger of a kind that never daunts the least courageous man, for love and pleasure followed it. The apprentice sleeping in the shop, the cook bivouacking in the kitchen, Perez and his wife sleeping, no doubt, the wakeful sleep of the aged, the echoing sonority of the old mansion, the close surveillance of the girl in the day-time,--all these things were obstacles, and made success a thing well-nigh impossible. But Montefiore had in his favor against all impossibilities the blood of the Maranas which gushed in the heart of that inquisitive girl, Italian by birth, Spanish in principles, virgin indeed, but impatient to love. Passion, the girl, and Montefiore were ready and able to defy the whole universe.

Montefiore, impelled as much by the instinct of a man of gallantry as by those vague hopes which cannot be explained, and to which we give the name of presentiments (a word of astonishing verbal accuracy), Montefiore spent the first hours of the night at his window, endeavoring to look below him to the secret apartment where, undoubtedly, the merchant and his wife had hidden the love and joyfulness of their old age. The ware-room of the "entresol" separated him from the rooms on the ground-floor. The captain therefore could not have recourse to noises significantly made from one floor to the other, an artificial language which all lovers know well how to create. But chance, or it may have been the young girl herself, came to his assistance. At the moment when he stationed himself at his window, he saw, on the black wall of the courtyard, a circle of light, in the centre of which the silhouette of Juana was clearly defined; the consecutive movement of the arms, and the attitude, gave evidence that she was arranging her hair for the night.

"Is she alone?" Montefiore asked himself; "could I, without danger, lower a letter filled with coin and strike it against that circular window in her hiding-place?"

At once he wrote a note, the note of a man exiled by his family to Elba, the note of a degraded marquis now a mere captain of equipment. Then he made a cord of whatever he could find that was capable of being turned into string, filled the note with a few silver crowns, and lowered it in the deepest silence to the centre of that spherical gleam.

"The shadows will show if her mother or the servant is with her," thought Montefiore. "If she is not alone, I can pull up the string at once."

But, after succeeding with infinite trouble in striking the glass, a single form, the little figure of Juana, appeared upon the wall. The young girl opened her window cautiously, saw the note, took it, and stood before the window while she read it. In it, Montefiore had given his name and asked for an interview, offering, after the style of the old romances, his heart and hand to the Signorina Juana di Mancini--a common trick, the success of which is nearly always certain. At Juana's age, nobility of soul increases the dangers which surround youth. A poet of our day has said: "Woman succumbs only to her own nobility. The lover pretends to doubt the love he inspires at the moment when he is most beloved; the young girl, confident and proud, longs to make sacrifices to prove her love, and knows the world and men too little to continue calm in the midst of her rising emotions and repel with contempt the man who accepts a life offered in expiation of a false reproach."

Ever since the constitution of societies the young girl finds herself torn by a struggle between the caution of prudent virtue and the evils of wrong-doing. Often she loses a love, delightful in prospect, and the first, if she resists; on the other hand, she loses a marriage if she is imprudent. Casting a glance over the vicissitudes of social life in Paris, it is impossible to doubt the necessity of religion; and yet Paris is situated in the forty-eighth degree of latitude, while Tarragona is in the forty-first. The old question of climates is still useful to narrators to explain the sudden denouements, the imprudences, or the resistances of love.

Montefiore kept his eyes fixed on the exquisite black profile projected by the gleam upon the wall. Neither he nor Juana could see each other; a troublesome cornice, vexatiously placed, deprived them of the mute correspondence which may be established between a pair of lovers as they bend to each other from their windows. Thus the mind and the attention of the captain were concentrated on that luminous circle where, without perhaps knowing it herself, the young girl would, he thought, innocently reveal her thoughts by a series of gestures. But no! The singular motions she proceeded to make gave not a particle of hope to the expectant lover. Juana was amusing herself by cutting up his missive. But virtue and innocence sometimes imitate the clever proceedings inspired by jealousy to the Bartholos of comedy. Juana, without pens, ink, or paper, was replying by snip of scissors. Presently she refastened the note to the string; the officer drew it up, opened it, and read by the light of his lamp one word, carefully cut out of the paper: COME.

"Come!" he said to himself; "but what of poison? or the dagger or carbine of Perez? And that apprentice not yet asleep, perhaps, in the shop? and the servant in her hammock? Besides, this old house echoes the slightest sound; I can hear old Perez snoring even here. Come, indeed! She can have nothing more to lose."

Bitter reflection! rakes alone are logical and will punish a woman for devotion. Man created Satan and Lovelace; but a virgin is an angel on whom he can bestow naught but his own vices. She is so grand, so beautiful, that he cannot magnify or embellish her; he has only the fatal power to blast her and drag her down into his own mire.

Montefiore waited for a later and more somnolent hour of the night; then, in spite of his reflections, he descended the stairs without boots, armed with his pistols, moving step by step, stopping to question the silence, putting forth his hands, measuring the stairs, peering into the darkness, and ready at the slightest incident to fly back into his room. The Italian had put on his handsomest uniform; he had perfumed his black hair, and now shone with the particular brilliancy which dress and toilet bestow upon natural beauty. Under such circumstances most men are as feminine as a woman.

The marquis arrived without hindrance before the secret door of the room in which the girl was hidden, a sort of cell made in the angle of the house and belonging exclusively to Juana, who had remained there hidden during the day from every eye while the siege lasted. Up to the present time she had slept in the room of her adopted mother, but the limited space in the garret where the merchant and his wife had gone to make room for the officer who was billeted upon them, did not allow of her going with them. Dona Lagounia had therefore left the young girl to the guardianship of lock and key, under the protection of religious ideas, all the more efficacious because they were partly superstitious, and also under the shield of a native pride and sensitive modesty which made the young Mancini in sort an exception among her sex. Juana possessed in an equal degree the most attaching virtues and the most passionate impulses; she had needed the modesty and sanctity of this monotonous life to calm and cool the tumultuous blood of the Maranas which bounded in her heart, the desires of which her adopted mother told her were an instigation of the devil.

A faint ray of light traced along the sill of the secret door guided Montefiore to the place; he scratched the panel softly and Juana opened to him. Montefiore entered, palpitating, but he recognized in the expression of the girl's face complete ignorance of her peril, a sort of naive curiosity, and an innocent admiration. He stopped short, arrested for a moment by the sacredness of the picture which met his eyes.

He saw before him a tapestry on the walls with a gray ground sprinkled with violets, a little coffer of ebony, an antique mirror, an immense and very old arm chair also in ebony and covered with tapestry, a table with twisted legs, a pretty carpet on the floor, near the table a single chair; and that was all. On the table, however, were flowers and embroidery; in a recess at the farther end of the room was the narrow little bed where Juana dreamed. Above the bed were three pictures; and near the pillow a crucifix, with a holy water basin and a prayer, printed in letters of gold and framed. Flowers exhaled their perfume faintly; the candles cast a tender light; all was calm and pure and sacred. The dreamy thoughts of Juana, but above all Juana herself, had communicated to all things her own peculiar charm; her soul appeared to shine there, like the pearl in its matrix. Juana, dressed in white, beautiful with naught but her own beauty, laying down her rosary to answer love, might have inspired respect, even in a Montefiore, if the silence, if the night, if Juana herself had not seemed so amorous. Montefiore stood still, intoxicated with an unknown happiness, possibly that of Satan beholding heaven through a rift of the clouds which form its enclosure.

"As soon as I saw you," he said in pure Tuscan, and in the modest tone of voice so peculiarly Italian, "I loved you. My soul and my life are now in you, and in you they will be forever, if you will have it so."

Juana listened, inhaling from the atmosphere the sound of these words which the accents of love made magnificent.

"Poor child! how have you breathed so long the air of this dismal house without dying of it? You, made to reign in the world, to inhabit the palace of a prince, to live in the midst of fetes, to feel the joys which love bestows, to see the world at your feet, to efface all other beauty by your own which can have no rival--you, to live here, solitary, with those two shopkeepers!"

Adroit question! He wished to know if Juana had a lover.

"True," she replied. "But who can have told you my secret thoughts? For the last few months I have nearly died of sadness. Yes, I would *rather* die than stay longer in this house. Look at that embroidery; there is not a stitch there which I did not set with dreadful thoughts. How many times I have thought of escaping to fling myself into the sea! Why? I don't know why,--little childish troubles, but very keen, though they are so silly. Often I have kissed my mother at night as one would kiss a mother for the last time, saying in my heart: 'To-morrow I will kill myself.' But I do not die. Suicides go to hell, you know, and I am so afraid of hell that I resign myself to live, to get up in the morning and go to bed at night, and work the same hours, and do the same things. I am not so weary of it, but I suffer--And yet, my father and mother adore me. Oh! I am bad, I am bad; I say so to my confessor."

"Do you always live here alone, without amusement, without pleasures?"

"Oh! I have not always been like this. Till I was fifteen the festivals of the church, the chants, the music gave me pleasure. I was happy, feeling myself like the angels without sin and able to communicate every week--I loved God then. But for the last three years, from day to day, all things have changed. First, I wanted flowers here--and I have them, lovely flowers! Then I wanted--but I want nothing now," she added, after a pause, smiling at Montefiore. "Have you not said that you would love me always?"

"Yes, my Juana," cried Montefiore, softly, taking her round the waist and pressing her to his heart, "yes. But let me speak to you as you speak to God. Are you not as beautiful as Mary in heaven? Listen. I swear to you," he continued, kissing her hair, "I swear to take that forehead for my altar, to make you my idol, to lay at your feet all the luxuries of the world. For you, my palace at Milan; for you my horses, my jewels, the diamonds of my ancient family; for you, each day, fresh jewels, a thousand pleasures, and all the joys of earth!"

"Yes," she said reflectively, "I would like that; but I feel within my soul that I would like better than all the world my husband. Mio caro sposo!" she said, as if it were impossible to give in any other language the infinite tenderness, the loving elegance with which the Italian tongue and accent clothe those delightful words. Besides, Italian was Juana's maternal language.

"I should find," she continued, with a glance at Montefiore in which shone the purity of the cherubim, "I should find in *him* my dear religion, him and God--God and him. Is he to be you?" she said. "Yes, surely it will be you," she cried, after a pause. "Come, and see the picture my father brought me from Italy."

She took a candle, made a sign to Montefiore, and showed him at the foot of her bed a Saint Michael overthrowing the demon.

"Look!" she said, "has he not your eyes? When I saw you from my window in the street, our meeting seemed to me a sign from heaven. Every day during my morning meditation, while waiting for my mother to call me to prayer, I have so gazed at that picture, that angel, that I have ended by thinking him my husband--oh! heavens, I speak to you as though you were myself. I must seem crazy to you; but if you only knew how a poor captive wants to tell the thoughts that choke her! When alone, I talk to my flowers, to my tapestry; they can understand me better, I think, than my father and mother, who are so grave."

"Juana," said Montefiore, taking her hands and kissing them with the passion that gushed in his eyes, in his gestures, in the tones of his voice, "speak to me as your husband, as yourself. I have suffered all that you have suffered. Between us two few words are needed to make us comprehend our past, but there will never be enough to express our coming happiness. Lay your hand upon my heart. Feel how it beats. Let us promise before God, who sees and hears us, to be faithful to each other throughout our lives. Here, take my ring--and give me yours."

"Give you my ring!" she said in terror.

"Why not?" asked Montefiore, uneasy at such artlessness.

"But our holy father the Pope has blessed it; it was put upon my finger in childhood by a beautiful lady who took care of me, and who told me never to part with it."

"Juana, you cannot love me!"

"Ah!" she said, "here it is; take it. You, are you not another myself?"

She held out the ring with a trembling hand, holding it tightly as she looked at Montefiore with a clear and penetrating eye that questioned him. That ring! all of herself was in it; but she gave it to him.

"Oh, my Juana!" said Montefiore, again pressing her in his arms. "I should be a monster indeed if I deceived you. I will love you forever."

Juana was thoughtful. Montefiore, reflecting that in this first interview he ought to venture upon nothing that might frighten a young girl so ignorantly pure, so imprudent by virtue rather than from desire, postponed all further action to the future, relying on his beauty, of which he knew the power, and on this innocent ring-marriage, the hymen of the heart, the lightest, yet the strongest of all ceremonies. For the rest of that night, and throughout the next day, Juana's imagination was the accomplice of her passion.

On this first evening Montefiore forced himself to be as respectful as he was tender. With that intention, in the interests of his passion and the desires with which Juana inspired him, he was caressing and unctuous in language; he launched the young creature into plans for a new existence, described to her the world under glowing colors, talked to her of household details always attractive to the mind of girls, giving her a sense of the rights and realities of love. Then, having agreed upon the hour for their future nocturnal interviews, he left her happy, but changed; the pure and pious Juana existed no longer; in the last glance she gave him, in the pretty movement by which she brought her forehead to his lips, there was already more of passion than a girl should feel. Solitude, weariness of employments contrary to her nature had brought this about. To make the daughter of the Maranas truly virtuous, she ought to have been habituated, little by little, to the world, or else to have been wholly withdrawn from it.

"The day, to-morrow, will seem very long to me," she said, receiving his kisses on her forehead. "But stay in the salon, and speak loud, that I may hear your voice; it fills my soul."

Montefiore, clever enough to imagine the girl's life, was all the more satisfied with himself for restraining his desires because he saw that it would lead to his greater contentment. He returned to his room without accident.

Ten days went by without any event occurring to trouble the peace and solitude of the house. Montefiore employed his Italian cajolery on old Perez, on Dona Lagounia, on the apprentice, even on the cook, and they all liked him; but, in spite of the confidence he now inspired in them, he never asked to see Juana, or to have the door of her mysterious hiding-place opened to him. The young girl, hungry to see her lover, implored him to do so; but he always refused her from an instinct of prudence. Besides, he had used his best powers and fascinations to lull the suspicions of the old couple, and had now accustomed them to see him, a soldier, stay in bed till midday on pretence that he was ill. Thus the lovers lived only in the night-time, when the rest of the household were asleep. If Montefiore had not been one of those libertines whom the habit of gallantry enables to retain their self-possession under all circumstances, he might have been lost a dozen times during those ten days. A young lover, in the simplicity of a first love, would have committed the enchanting imprudences which are so difficult to resist. But he did resist even Juana herself, Juana pouting, Juana making her long hair a chain which she wound about his neck when caution told him he must go.

The most suspicious of guardians would however have been puzzled to detect the secret of their nightly meetings. It is to be supposed that, sure of success, the Italian marquis gave himself the ineffable pleasures of a slow seduction, step by step, leading gradually to the fire which should end the affair in a conflagration. On the eleventh day, at the dinner-table, he thought it wise to inform old Perez, under seal of secrecy, that the reason of his separation from his family was an ill-assorted marriage. This false revelation was an infamous thing in view of the nocturnal drama which was being played under that roof. Montefiore, an experienced rake, was preparing for the finale of that drama which he foresaw and enjoyed as an artist who loves his art. He expected to leave before long, and without regret, the house and his love. It would happen, he thought, in this way: Juana, after waiting for him in vain for several nights, would risk her life, perhaps, in asking Perez what had become of his guest; and Perez would reply, not aware of the importance of his answer,--

"The Marquis de Montefiore is reconciled to his family, who consent to receive his wife; he has gone to Italy to present her to them."

And Juana?--The marquis never asked himself what would become of Juana; but he had studied her character, its nobility, candor, and strength, and he knew he might be sure of her silence.

He obtained a mission from one of the generals. Three days later, on the night preceding his intended departure, Montefiore, instead of returning to his own room after dinner, contrived to enter unseen that of Juana, to make that farewell night the longer. Juana, true Spaniard and true Italian, was enchanted with such boldness; it argued ardor! For herself she did not fear discovery. To find in the pure love of marriage the excitements of intrigue, to hide her husband behind the curtains of her bed, and say to her adopted father and mother, in case of detection: "I am the Marquise de Montefiore!"--was to an ignorant and romantic young girl, who for three years past had dreamed of love without dreaming of its dangers, delightful. The door closed on this last evening upon her folly, her happiness, like a veil, which it is useless here to raise.

It was nine o'clock; the merchant and his wife were reading their evening prayers; suddenly the noise of a carriage drawn by several horses resounded in the street; loud and hasty raps echoed from the shop where the servant hurried to open the door, and into that venerable salon rushed a woman, magnificently dressed in spite of the mud upon the wheels of her travelling-carriage, which had just crossed Italy, France, and Spain. It was, of course, the Marana,--the Marana who, in spite of her thirty-six years, was still in all the glory of her ravishing beauty; the Marana who, being at that time the mistress of a king, had left Naples, the fetes, the skies of Naples, the climax of her life of luxury, on hearing from her royal lover of the events in Spain and the siege of Tarragona.

"Tarragona! I must get to Tarragona before the town is taken!" she cried. "Ten days to reach Tarragona!"

Then without caring for crown or court, she arrived in Tarragona, furnished with an almost imperial safe-conduct; furnished too with gold which enabled her to cross France with the velocity of a rocket.

"My daughter! my daughter!" cried the Marana.

At this voice, and the abrupt invasion of their solitude, the prayer-book fell from the hands of the old couple.

"She is there," replied the merchant, calmly, after a pause during which he recovered from the emotion caused by the abrupt entrance, and the look and voice of the mother. "She is there," he repeated, pointing to the door of the little chamber.

"Yes, but has any harm come to her; is she still--"

"Perfectly well," said Dona Lagounia.

"O God! send me to hell if it so pleases thee!" cried the Marana, dropping, exhausted and half dead, into a chair.

The flush in her cheeks, due to anxiety, paled suddenly; she had strength to endure suffering, but none to bear this joy. Joy was more violent in her soul than suffering, for it contained the echoes of her pain and the agonies of its own emotion.

"But," she said, "how have you kept her safe? Tarragona is taken."

"Yes," said Perez, "but since you see me living why do you ask that question? Should I not have died before harm could have come to Juana?"

At that answer, the Marana seized the calloused hand of the old man, and kissed it, wetting it with the tears that flowed from her eyes --she who never wept! those tears were all she had most precious under heaven.

"My good Perez!" she said at last. "But have you had no soldiers quartered in your house?"

"Only one," replied the Spaniard. "Fortunately for us the most loyal of men; a Spaniard by birth, but now an Italian who hates Bonaparte; a married man. He is ill, and gets up late and goes to bed early."

"An Italian! What is his name?"

"Montefiore."

"Can it be the Marquis de Montefiore--"

"Yes, Senora, he himself."

"Has he seen Juana?"

"No," said Dona Lagounia.

"You are mistaken, wife," said Perez. "The marquis must have seen her for a moment, a short moment, it is true; but I think he looked at her that evening she came in here during supper."

"Ah, let me see my daughter!"

"Nothing easier," said Perez; "she is now asleep. If she has left the key in the lock we must waken her."

As he rose to take the duplicate key of Juana's door his eyes fell by chance on the circular gleam of light upon the black wall of the inner courtyard. Within that circle he saw the shadow of a group such as Canova alone has attempted to render. The Spaniard turned back.

"I do not know," he said to the Marana, "where to find the key."

"You are very pale," she said.

"And I will show you why," he cried, seizing his dagger and rapping its hilt violently on Juana's door as he shouted,--

"Open! open! open! Juana!"

Juana did not open, for she needed time to conceal Montefiore. She knew nothing of what was passing in the salon; the double portieres of thick tapestry deadened all sounds.

"Madame, I lied to you in saying I could not find the key. Here it is," added Perez, taking it from a sideboard. "But it is useless. Juana's key is in the lock; her door is barricaded. We have been deceived, my wife!" he added, turning to Dona Lagounia. "There is a man in Juana's room."

"Impossible! By my eternal salvation I say it is impossible!" said his wife.

"Do not swear, Dona Lagounia. Our honor is dead, and this woman--" He pointed to the Marana, who had risen and was standing motionless, blasted by his words, "this woman has the right to despise us. She saved our life, our fortune, and our honor, and we have saved nothing for her but her money--Juana!" he cried again, "open, or I will burst in your door."

His voice, rising in violence, echoed through the garrets in the roof. He was cold and calm. The life of Montefiore was in his hands; he would wash away his remorse in the blood of that Italian.

"Out, out, out! out, all of you!" cried the Marana, springing like a

tigress on the dagger, which she wrenched from the hand of the aston-
ished Perez. "Out, Perez," she continued more calmly, "out, you and
your wife and servants! There will be murder here. You might be shot
by the French. Have nothing to do with this; it is my affair, mine only.
Between my daughter and me there is none but God. As for the man,
he belongs to *me*. The whole earth could not tear him from my grasp.
Go, go! I forgive you. I see plainly that the girl is a Marana. You, your
religion, your virtue, were too weak to fight against my blood."

She gave a dreadful sigh, turning her dry eyes on them. She had lost
all, but she knew how to suffer,--a true courtesan.

The door opened. The Marana forgot all else, and Perez, making
a sign to his wife, remained at his post. With his old invincible Spanish honor he was determined to share the vengeance of the betrayed
mother. Juana, all in white, and softly lighted by the wax candles, was
standing calmly in the centre of her chamber.

"What do you want with me?" she said.

The Marana could not repress a passing shudder.

"Perez," she asked, "has this room another issue?"

Perez made a negative gesture; confiding in that gesture, the mother
entered the room.

"Juana," she said, "I am your mother, your judge; you have placed
yourself in the only situation in which I could reveal myself to you. You
have come down to me, you, whom I thought in heaven. Ah! you have
fallen low indeed. You have a lover in this room."

"Madame, there is and can be no one but my husband," answered
the girl. "I am the Marquise de Montefiore."

"Then there are two," said Perez, in a grave voice. "He told me he
was married."

"Montefiore, my love!" cried the girl, tearing aside the curtain and revealing the officer. "Come! they are slandering you."

The Italian appeared, pale and speechless; he saw the dagger in the Marana's hand, and he knew her well. With one bound he sprang from the room, crying out in a thundering voice,--

"Help! help! they are murdering a Frenchman. Soldiers of the 6th of the line, rush for Captain Diard! Help, help!"

Perez had gripped the man and was trying to gag him with his large hand, but the Marana stopped him, saying,--

"Bind him fast, but let him shout. Open the doors, leave them open, and go, go, as I told you; go, all of you.--As for you," she said, addressing Montefiore, "shout, call for help if you choose; by the time your soldiers get here this blade will be in your heart. Are you married? Answer."

Montefiore, who had fallen on the threshold of the door, scarcely a step from Juana, saw nothing but the blade of the dagger, the gleam of which blinded him.

"Has he deceived me?" said Juana, slowly. "He told me he was free."

"He told me that he was married," repeated Perez, in his solemn voice.

"Holy Virgin!" murmured Dona Lagounia.

"Answer, soul of corruption," said the Marana, in a low voice, bending to the ear of the marquis.

"Your daughter--" began Montefiore.

"The daughter that was mine is dead or dying," interrupted the Marana. "I have no daughter; do not utter that word. Answer, are you married?"

"No, madame," said Montefiore, at last, striving to gain time, "I desire to marry your daughter."

"My noble Montefiore!" said Juana, drawing a deep breath.

"Then why did you attempt to fly and cry for help?" asked Perez.

Terrible, revealing light!

Juana said nothing, but she wrung her hands and went to her arm-chair and sat down.

At that moment a tumult rose in the street which was plainly heard in the silence of the room. A soldier of the 6th, hearing Montefiore's cry for help, had summoned Diard. The quartermaster, who was fortunately in his bivouac, came, accompanied by friends.

"Why did I fly?" said Montefiore, hearing the voice of his friend. "Because I told you the truth; I am married--Diard! Diard!" he shouted in a piercing voice.

But, at a word from Perez, the apprentice closed and bolted the doors, so that the soldiers were delayed by battering them in. Before they could enter, the Marana had time to strike her dagger into the guilty man; but anger hindered her aim, the blade slipped upon the Italian's epaulet, though she struck her blow with such force that he fell at the very feet of Juana, who took no notice of him. The Marana sprang upon him, and this time, resolved not to miss her prey, she caught him by the throat.

"I am free and I will marry her! I swear it, by God, by my mother, by all there is most sacred in the world; I am a bachelor; I will marry her, on my honor!"

And he bit the arm of the courtesan.

"Mother," said Juana, "kill him. He is so base that I will not have him for my husband, were he ten times as beautiful."

"Ah! I recognize my daughter!" cried the mother.

"What is all this?" demanded the quartermaster, entering the room.

"They are murdering me," cried Montefiore, "on account of this girl; she says I am her lover. She inveigled me into a trap, and they are forcing me to marry her--"

"And you reject her?" cried Diard, struck with the splendid beauty which contempt, hatred, and indignation had given to the girl, already so beautiful. "Then you are hard to please. If she wants a husband I am ready to marry her. Put up your weapons; there is no trouble here."

The Marana pulled the Italian to the side of her daughter's bed and said to him, in a low voice,--

"If I spare you, give thanks for the rest of your life; but, remember this, if your tongue ever injures my daughter you will see me again. Go!--How much 'dot' do you give her?" she continued, going up to Perez.

"She has two hundred thousand gold piastres," replied the Spaniard.

"And that is not all, monsieur," said the Marana, turning to Diard. "Who are you?--Go!" she repeated to Montefiore.

The marquis, hearing this statement of gold piastres, came forward once more, saying,--

"I am really free--"

A glance from Juana silenced him.

"You are really free to go," she said.

And he went immediately.

"Alas! monsieur," said the girl, turning to Diard, "I thank you with admiration. But my husband is in heaven. To-morrow I shall enter a convent--"

"Juana, my Juana, hush!" cried the mother, clasping her in her arms. Then she whispered in the girl's ear. "You *must* have another husband."

Juana turned pale. She freed herself from her mother and sat down once more in her arm-chair.

"Who are you, monsieur?" repeated the Marana, addressing Diard.

"Madame, I am at present only the quartermaster of the 6th of the line. But for such a wife I have the heart to make myself a marshal of France. My name is Pierre-Francois Diard. My father was provost of merchants. I am not--"

"But, at least, you are an honest man, are you not?" cried the Marana, interrupting him. "If you please the Signorina Juana di Mancini, you can marry her and be happy together.--Juana," she continued in a grave tone, "in becoming the wife of a brave and worthy man remember that you will also be a mother. I have sworn that you shall kiss your children without a blush upon your face" (her voice faltered slightly). "I have sworn that you shall live a virtuous life; expect, therefore, many troubles. But, whatever happens, continue pure, and be faithful to your husband. Sacrifice all things to him, for he will be the father of your children--the father of your children! If you take a lover, I, your mother, will stand between you and him. Do you see that dagger? It is in your 'dot,'" she continued, throwing the weapon on Juana's bed. "I leave it there as the guarantee of your honor so long as my eyes are open and my arm free. Farewell," she said, restraining her tears. "God grant that we may never meet again."

At that idea, her tears began to flow.

"Poor child!" she added, "you have been happier than you knew in this dull home.--Do not allow her to regret it," she said, turning to Diard.

The foregoing rapid narrative is not the principal subject of this Study, for the understanding of which it was necessary to explain how it happened that the quartermaster Diard married Juana di Mancini, that Montefiore and Diard were intimately known to each other, and to show plainly what blood and what passions were in Madame Diard.

CHAPTER III
THE HISTORY OF MADAME DIARD

By the time that the quartermaster had fulfilled all the long and dilatory formalities without which no French soldier can be married, he was passionately in love with Juana di Mancini, and Juana had had time to think of her coming destiny.

An awful destiny! Juana, who felt neither esteem nor love for Diard, was bound to him forever, by a rash but necessary promise. The man was neither handsome nor well-made. His manners, devoid of all distinction, were a mixture of the worst army tone, the habits of his province, and his own insufficient education. How could she love Diard, she, a young girl all grace and elegance, born with an invincible instinct for luxury and good taste, her very nature tending toward the sphere of the higher social classes? As for esteeming him, she rejected the very thought precisely because he had married her. This repulsion was natural. Woman is a saintly and noble creature, but almost always misunderstood, and nearly always misjudged because she is misunderstood. If Juana had loved Diard she would have esteemed him. Love creates in a wife a new woman; the woman of the day before no longer exists on the morrow. Putting on the nuptial robe of a passion in which life itself is concerned, the woman wraps herself in purity and whiteness. Reborn into virtue and chastity, there is no past for her; she is all future, and should forget the things behind her to relearn life. In this sense the famous words which a modern poet has put into the lips of Marion Delorme is infused with truth,--

"And Love remade me virgin."

That line seems like a reminiscence of a tragedy of Corneille, so truly does it recall the energetic diction of the father of our modern theatre. Yet the poet was forced to sacrifice it to the essentially vaudevillist spirit of the pit.

So Juana loveless was doomed to be Juana humiliated, degraded, hopeless. She could not honor the man who took her thus. She felt, in all the conscientious purity of her youth, that distinction, subtle in appearance but sacredly true, legal with the heart's legality, which women apply instinctively to all their feelings, even the least reflective. Juana became profoundly sad as she saw the nature and the extent of the life before her. Often she turned her eyes, brimming with tears proudly repressed, upon Perez and Dona Lagounia, who fully comprehended, both of them, the bitter thoughts those tears contained. But they were silent: of what good were reproaches now; why look for consolations? The deeper they were, the more they enlarged the wound.

One evening, Juana, stupid with grief, heard through the open door of her little room, which the old couple had thought shut, a pitying moan from her adopted mother.

"The child will die of grief."

"Yes," said Perez, in a shaking voice, "but what can we do? I cannot now boast of her beauty and her chastity to Comte d'Arcos, to whom I hoped to marry her."

"But a single fault is not vice," said the old woman, pitying as the angels.

"Her mother gave her to this man," said Perez.

"Yes, in a moment; without consulting the poor child!" cried Dona Lagounia.

"She knew what she was doing."

"But oh! into what hands our pearl is going!"

"Say no more, or I shall seek a quarrel with that Diard."

"And that would only lead to other miseries."

Hearing these dreadful words Juana saw the happy future she had lost by her own wrongdoing. The pure and simple years of her quiet life would have been rewarded by a brilliant existence such as she had fondly dreamed,--dreams which had caused her ruin. To fall from the height of Greatness to Monsieur Diard! She wept. At times she went nearly mad. She floated for a while between vice and religion. Vice was a speedy solution, religion a lifetime of suffering. The meditation was stormy and solemn. The next day was the fatal day, the day for the marriage. But Juana could still remain free. Free, she knew how far her misery would go; married, she was ignorant of where it went or what it might bring her.

Religion triumphed. Dona Lagounia stayed beside her child and prayed and watched as she would have prayed and watched beside the dying.

"God wills it," she said to Juana.

Nature gives to woman alternately a strength which enables her to suffer and a weakness which leads her to resignation. Juana resigned herself; and without restriction. She determined to obey her mother's prayer, and cross the desert of life to reach God's heaven, knowing well that no flowers grew for her along the way of that painful journey.

She married Diard. As for the quartermaster, though he had no grace in Juana's eyes, we may well absolve him. He loved her distractedly. The Marana, so keen to know the signs of love, had recognized in that man the accents of passion and the brusque nature, the generous impulses, that are common to Southerners. In the paroxysm of her anger and her distress she had thought such qualities enough for her daughter's happiness.

The first days of this marriage were apparently happy; or, to express one of those latent facts, the miseries of which are buried by women in the depths of their souls, Juana would not cast down her husband's joy,--a double role, dreadful to play, but to which, sooner or later, all women unhappily married come. This is a history impossible to recount in its full truth. Juana, struggling hourly against her nature, a nature both Spanish and Italian, having dried up the source of her tears by dint of weeping, was a human type, destined to represent woman's misery in its utmost expression, namely, sorrow undyingly active; the description of which would need such minute observations that to persons eager for dramatic emotions they would seem insipid. This analysis, in which every wife would find some one of her own sufferings, would require a volume to express them all; a fruitless, hopeless volume by its very nature, the merit of which would consist in faintest tints and delicate shadings which critics would declare to be effeminate and diffuse. Besides, what man could rightly approach, unless he bore another heart within his heart, those solemn and touching elegies which certain women carry with them to their tomb; melancholies, misunderstood even by those who cause them; sighs unheeded, devotions unrewarded,--on earth at least,--splendid silences misconstrued; vengeances withheld, disdained; generosities perpetually bestowed and wasted; pleasures longed for and denied; angelic charities secretly accomplished,--in short, all the religions of womanhood and its inextinguishable love.

Juana knew that life; fate spared her nought. She was wholly a wife, but a sorrowful and suffering wife; a wife incessantly wounded, yet forgiving always; a wife pure as a flawless diamond,--she who had the beauty and the glow of the diamond, and in that beauty, that glow, a vengeance in her hand; for she was certainly not a woman to fear the dagger added to her "dot."

At first, inspired by a real love, by one of those passions which for the time being change even odious characters and bring to light all that may be noble in a soul, Diard behaved like a man of honor. He forced Montefiore to leave the regiment and even the army corps, so that his wife might never meet him during the time they remained in Spain. Next, he petitioned for his own removal, and succeeded in entering the Imperial Guard. He desired at any price to obtain a title, honors, and consideration in keeping with his present wealth. With this idea in his mind, he behaved courageously in one of the most bloody battles in Germany, but, unfortunately, he was too severely wounded to remain in the service. Threatened with the loss of a leg, he was forced to retire on a pension, without the title of baron, without those rewards he hoped to win, and would have won had he not been Diard.

This event, this wound, and his thwarted hopes contributed to change his character. His Provencal energy, roused for a time, sank down. At first he was sustained by his wife, in whom his efforts, his courage, his ambition had induced some belief in his nature, and who showed herself, what women are, tender and consoling in the troubles of life. Inspired by a few words from Juana, the retired soldier came to Paris, resolved to win in an administrative career a position to command respect, bury in oblivion the quartermaster of the 6th of the line, and secure for Madame Diard a noble title. His passion for that seductive creature enabled him to divine her most secret wishes. Juana expressed nothing, but he understood her. He was not loved as a lover dreams of being loved; he knew this, and he strove to make himself respected, loved, and cherished. He foresaw a coming happiness, poor man, in the patience and gentleness shown on all occasions by his wife; but that patience, that gentleness, were only the outward signs of the resignation which had made her his wife. Resignation, religion, were they love? Often Diard wished for refusal where he met with chaste obedience; often he would have given his eternal life that Juana might have wept upon his bosom and not disguised her secret thoughts behind a smiling face which lied to him nobly. Many young men --for after a certain age men no longer struggle--persist in the effort to triumph over an evil fate, the thunder of which they hear, from time to time, on the horizon of their lives; and when at last they succumb and roll down the precipice of evil, we ought to do them justice and acknowledge these inward struggles.

Like many men Diard tried all things, and all things were hostile to him. His wealth enabled him to surround his wife with the enjoyments of Parisian luxury. She lived in a fine house, with noble rooms, where she maintained a salon, in which abounded artists (by nature no judges of men), men of pleasure ready to amuse themselves anywhere, a few politicians who swelled the numbers, and certain men of fashion, all of whom admired Juana. Those who put themselves before the eyes of the public in Paris must either conquer Paris or be subject to it. Diard's character was not sufficiently strong, compact, or persistent to command society at that epoch, because it was an epoch when all men were endeavoring to rise. Social classifications ready-made are perhaps a great boon even for the people. Napoleon has confided to us the pains he took to inspire respect in his court, where most of the courtiers had been his equals. But Napoleon was Corsican, and Diard Provencal. Given equal genius, an islander will always be more compact and rounded than the man of terra firma in the same latitude; the arm of the sea which separates Corsica from Provence is, in spite of human science, an ocean which has made two nations.

Diard's mongrel position, which he himself made still more questionable, brought him great troubles. Perhaps there is useful instruction to be derived from the almost imperceptible connection of acts which led to the finale of this history.

In the first place, the sneerers of Paris did not see without malicious smiles and words the pictures with which the former quartermaster adorned his handsome mansion. Works of art purchased the night before were said to be spoils from Spain; and this accusation was the revenge of those who were jealous of his present fortune. Juana comprehended this reproach, and by her advice Diard sent back to Tarragona all the pictures he had brought from there. But the public, determined to see things in the worst light, only said, "That Diard is shrewd; he has sold his pictures." Worthy people continued to think that those which remained in the Diard salons were not honorably acquired. Some jealous women asked how it was that a *Diard* (!) had been able to marry so rich and beautiful a young girl. Hence comments and satires without end, such as Paris contributes. And yet, it must be said, that Juana met on all sides the respect inspired by her pure and religious life, which triumphed over everything, even Parisian calumny; but this respect stopped short with her, her husband received none of it. Juana's feminine perception and her keen eye hovering over her salons, brought her nothing but pain.

This lack of esteem was perfectly natural. Diard's comrades, in spite of the virtues which our imaginations attribute to soldiers, never forgave the former quartermaster of the 6th of the line for becoming suddenly so rich and for attempting to cut a figure in Paris. Now in Paris, from the last house in the faubourg Saint-Germain to the last in the rue Saint-Lazare, between the heights of the Luxembourg and the heights of Montmartre, all that clothes itself and gabbles, clothes itself to go out and goes out to gabble. All that world of great and small pretensions, that world of insolence and humble desires, of envy and cringing, all that is gilded or tarnished, young or old, noble of yesterday or noble from the fourth century, all that sneers at a parvenu, all that fears to commit itself, all that wants to demolish power and worships power if it resists,-- *all* those ears hear, *all* those tongues say, *all* those minds know, in a single evening, where the new-comer who aspires to honor among them was born and brought up, and what that interloper has done, or has not done, in the course of his life. There may be no court of assizes for the upper classes of society; but at any rate they have the most cruel of public prosecutors, an intangible moral being, both judge and executioner, who accuses and brands. Do not hope to hide anything from him; tell him all yourself; he wants to know all and he will know all. Do not ask what mysterious telegraph it was which conveyed to him in the twinkling of an eye, at any hour, in any place, that story, that bit of news, that scandal; do not ask what prompts him. That telegraph is a social mystery; no observer can report its effects. Of many extraordinary instances thereof, one may suffice: The assassination of the Duc de Berry, which occurred at the Opera-house, was related within ten minutes in the Ile-Saint-Louis. Thus the opinion of the 6th of the line as to its quartermaster filtered through society the night on which he gave his first ball.

Diard was therefore debarred from succeeding in society. Henceforth his wife alone had the power to make anything of him. Miracle of our strange civilization! In Paris, if a man is incapable of being anything himself, his wife, when she is young and clever, may give him other chances for elevation. We sometimes meet with invalid women, feeble beings apparently, who, without rising from sofas or leaving their chambers, have ruled society, moved a thousand springs, and placed their husbands where their ambition or their vanity prompted. But Juana, whose childhood was passed in her retreat in Tarragona, knew nothing of the vices, the meannesses, or the resources of Parisian society; she looked at that society with the curiosity of a girl, but she learned from it only that which her sorrow and her wounded pride revealed to her.

Juana had the tact of a virgin heart which receives impressions in advance of the event, after the manner of what are called "sensitives." The solitary young girl, so suddenly become a woman and a wife, saw plainly that were she to attempt to compel society to respect her husband, it must be after the manner of Spanish beggars, carbine in hand. Besides, the multiplicity of the precautions she would have to take, would they meet the necessity? Suddenly she divined society as, once before, she had divined life, and she saw nothing around her but the immense extent of an irreparable disaster. She had, moreover, the additional grief of tardily recognizing her husband's peculiar form of incapacity; he was a man unfitted for any purpose that required continuity of ideas. He could not understand a consistent part, such as he ought to play in the world; he perceived it neither as a whole nor in its gradations, and its gradations were everything. He was in one of those positions where shrewdness and tact might have taken the place of strength; when shrewdness and tact succeed, they are, perhaps, the highest form of strength.

Now Diard, far from arresting the spot of oil on his garments left by his antecedents, did his best to spread it. Incapable of studying the phase of the empire in the midst of which he came to live in Paris, he wanted to be made prefect. At that time every one believed in the genius of Napoleon; his favor enhanced the value of all offices. Prefectures, those miniature empires, could only be filled by men of great names, or chamberlains of H.M. the emperor and king. Already the prefects were a species of vizier. The myrmidons of the great man scoffed at Diard's pretensions to a prefecture, whereupon he lowered his demand to a sub-prefecture. There was, of course, a ridiculous discrepancy between this latter demand and the magnitude of his fortune. To frequent the imperial salons and live with insolent luxury, and then to abandon that millionaire life and bury himself as sub-prefect at Issoudun or Savenay was certainly holding himself below his position. Juana, too late aware of our laws and habits and administrative customs, did not enlighten her husband soon enough. Diard, desperate, petitioned successively all the ministerial powers; repulsed everywhere, he found nothing open to him; and society then judged him as the government judged him and as he judged himself. Diard, grievously wounded on the battlefield, was nevertheless not decorated; the quartermaster, rich as he was, was allowed no place in public life, and society logically refused him that to which he pretended in its midst.

Finally, to cap all, the luckless man felt in his own home the superiority of his wife. Though she used great tact--we might say velvet softness if the term were admissible--to disguise from her husband this supremacy, which surprised and humiliated herself, Diard ended by being affected by it.

At a game of life like this men are either unmanned, or they grow the stronger, or they give themselves to evil. The courage or the ardor of this man lessened under the reiterated blows which his own faults dealt to his self-appreciation, and fault after fault he committed. In the first place he had to struggle against his own habits and character. A passionate Provencal, frank in his vices as in his virtues, this man whose fibres vibrated like the strings of a harp, was all heart to his former friends. He succored the shabby and spattered man as readily as the needy of rank; in short, he accepted everybody, and gave his hand in his gilded salons to many a poor devil. Observing this on one occasion, a general of the empire, a variety of the human species of which no type will presently remain, refused his hand to Diard, and called him, insolently, "my good fellow" when he met him. The few persons of really good society whom Diard knew, treated him with that elegant, polished contempt against which a new-made man has seldom any weapons. The manners, the semi-Italian gesticulations, the speech of Diard, his style of dress, --all contributed to repulse the respect which careful observation of matters of good taste and dignity might otherwise obtain for vulgar persons; the yoke of such conventionalities can only be cast off by great and un-thinkable powers. So goes the world.

These details but faintly picture the many tortures to which Jua-na was subjected; they came upon her one by one; each social nature pricked her with its own particular pin; and to a soul which preferred the thrust of a dagger, there could be no worse suffering than this struggle in which Diard received insults he did not feel and Juana felt those she did not receive. A moment came, an awful moment, when she gained a clear and lucid perception of society, and felt in one instant all the sor-rows which were gathering themselves together to fall upon her head. She judged her husband incapable of rising to the honored ranks of the social order, and she felt that he would one day descend to where his instincts led him. Henceforth Juana felt pity for him.

The future was very gloomy for this young woman. She lived in constant apprehension of some disaster. This presentiment was in her soul as a contagion is in the air, but she had strength of mind and will to disguise her anguish beneath a smile. Juana had ceased to think of

herself. She used her influence to make Diard resign his various pretensions and to show him, as a haven, the peaceful and consoling life of
home. Evils came from society--why not banish it? In his home Diard
found peace and respect; he reigned there. She felt herself strong to ac-
cept the trying task of making him happy,--he, a man dissatisfied with
himself. Her energy increased with the difficulties of life; she had all
the secret heroism necessary to her position; religion inspired her with
those desires which support the angel appointed to protect a Christian
soul--occult poesy, allegorical image of our two natures!

Diard abandoned his projects, closed his house to the world, and
lived in his home. But here he found another reef. The poor soldier had
one of those eccentric souls which need perpetual motion. Diard was
one of the men who are instinctively compelled to start again the moment they arrive, and whose vital object seems to be to come and go
incessantly, like the wheels mentioned in Holy Writ. Perhaps he felt
the need of flying from himself. Without wearying of Juana, without
blaming Juana, his passion for her, rendered tranquil by time, allowed
his natural character to assert itself. Henceforth his days of gloom were
more frequent, and he often gave way to southern excitement. The more
virtuous a woman is and the more irreproachable, the more a man likes
to find fault with her, if only to assert by that act his legal superiority.
But if by chance she seems really imposing to him, he feels the need of
foisting faults upon her. After that, between man and wife, trifles increase and grow till they swell to Alps.

But Juana, patient and without pride, gentle and without that bitter-
ness which women know so well how to cast into their submission, left
Diard no chance for planned ill-humor. Besides, she was one of those
noble creatures to whom it is impossible to speak disrespectfully; her
glance, in which her life, saintly and pure, shone out, had the weight

of a fascination. Diard, embarrassed at first, then annoyed, ended by feeling that such high virtue was a yoke upon him. The goodness of his wife gave him no violent emotions, and violent emotions were what he wanted. What myriads of scenes are played in the depths of his souls, beneath the cold exterior of lives that are, apparently, commonplace! Among these dramas, lasting each but a short time, though they influence life so powerfully and are frequently the forerunners of the great misfortune doomed to fall on so many marriages, it is difficult to choose an example. There was a scene, however, which particularly marked the moment when in the life of this husband and wife estrangement began. Perhaps it may also serve to explain the finale of this narrative.

Juana had two children, happily for her, two sons. The first was born seven months after her marriage. He was called Juan, and he strongly resembled his mother. The second was born about two years after her arrival in Paris. The latter resembled both Diard and Juana, but more particularly Diard. His name was Francisque. For the last five years Francisque had been the object of Juana's most tender and watchful care. The mother was constantly occupied with that child; to him her prettiest caresses; to him the toys, but to him, especially, the penetrating mother-looks. Juana had watched him from his cradle; she had studied his cries, his motions; she endeavored to discern his nature that she might educate him wisely. It seemed at times as if she had but that one child. Diard, seeing that the eldest, Juan, was in a way neglected, took him under his own protection; and without inquiring even of himself whether the boy was the fruit of that ephemeral love to which he owed his wife, he made him his Benjamin.

Of all the sentiments transmitted to her through the blood of her grandmothers which consumed her, Madame Diard accepted one alone, --maternal love. But she loved her children doubly: first with the noble violence of which her mother the Marana had given her the example; secondly, with grace and purity, in the spirit of those social virtues the practice of which was the glory of her life and her inward recompense. The secret thought, the conscience of her motherhood, which gave to the Marana's life its stamp of untaught poesy, was to Juana an acknowledged life, an open consolation at all hours. Her mother had been virtuous as other women are criminal,--in secret; she had stolen a fancied happiness, she had never really tasted it. But Juana, unhappy in her virtue as her mother was unhappy in her vice, could enjoy at all moments the ineffable delights which her mother had so craved and could not have. To her, as to her mother, maternity comprised all earthly sentiments. Each, from differing causes, had no other comfort in their misery. Juana's maternal love may have been the strongest because, deprived of all other affections, she put the joys she lacked into the one joy of her children; and there are noble passions that resemble vice; the more they are satisfied the more they increase. Mothers and gamblers are alike insatiable.

When Juana saw the generous pardon laid silently on the head of Juan by Diard's fatherly affection, she was much moved, and from the day when the husband and wife changed parts she felt for him the true and deep interest she had hitherto shown to him as a matter of duty only. If that man had been more consistent in his life; if he had not destroyed by fitful inconstancy and restlessness the forces of a true though excitable sensibility, Juana would doubtless have loved him in the end. Unfortunately, he was a type of those southern natures which are keen in perceptions they cannot follow out; capable of great things overnight, and incapable the next morning; often the victim of their own virtues, and often lucky through their worst passions; admirable men in some respects, when their good qualities are kept to a steady energy by some outward bond. For two years after his retreat from active life Diard was held captive in his home by the softest chains. He lived, almost in spite of himself, under the influence of his wife, who made herself gay and amusing to cheer him, who used the resources of feminine genius to attract and seduce him to a love of virtue, but whose ability and cleverness did not go so far as to simulate love.

At this time all Paris was talking of the affair of a captain in the army who in a paroxysm of libertine jealousy had killed a woman. Diard, on coming home to dinner, told his wife that the officer was dead. He had killed himself to avoid the dishonor of a trial and the shame of death upon the scaffold. Juana did not see at first the logic of such conduct, and her husband was obliged to explain to her the fine jurisprudence of French law, which does not prosecute the dead.

"But, papa, didn't you tell us the other day that the king could pardon?" asked Francisque.

"The king can give nothing but life," said Juan, half scornfully.

Diard and Juana, the spectators of this little scene, were differently affected by it. The glance, moist with joy, which his wife cast upon her eldest child was a fatal revelation to the husband of the secrets of a heart hitherto impenetrable. That eldest child was all Juana; Juana comprehended him; she was sure of his heart, his future; she adored him, but her ardent love was a secret between herself, her child, and God. Juan instinctively enjoyed the seeming indifference of his mother in presence of his father and brother, for she pressed him to her heart when alone. Francisque was Diard, and Juana's incessant care and watchfulness betrayed her desire to correct in the son the vices of the father and to encourage his better qualities. Juana, unaware that her glance had said too much and that her husband had rightly interpreted it, took Francisque in her lap and gave him, in a gentle voice still trembling with the pleasure that Juan's answer had brought her, a lesson upon honor, simplified to his childish intelligence.

"That boy's character requires care," said Diard.

"Yes," she replied simply.

"How about Juan?"

Madame Diard, struck by the tone in which the words were uttered, looked at her husband.

"Juan was born perfect," he added.

Then he sat down gloomily, and reflected. Presently, as his wife continued silent, he added:--

"You love one of *your* children better than the other."

"You know that," she said.

"No," said Diard, "I did not know until now which of them you preferred."

"But neither of them have ever given me a moment's uneasiness," she answered quickly.

"But one of them gives you greater joys," he said, more quickly still.

"I never counted them," she said.

"How false you women are!" cried Diard. "Will you dare to say that Juan is not the child of your heart?"

"If that were so," she said, with dignity, "do you think it a misfortune?"

"You have never loved me. If you had chosen, I would have conquered worlds for your sake. You know all that I have struggled to do in life, supported by the hope of pleasing you. Ah! if you had only loved me!"

"A woman who loves," said Juana, "likes to live in solitude, far from the world, and that is what we are doing."

"I know, Juana, that *you* are never in the wrong."

The words were said bitterly, and cast, for the rest of their lives together, a coldness between them.

On the morrow of that fatal day Diard went back to his old companions and found distractions for his mind in play. Unfortunately, he won much money, and continued playing. Little by little, he returned to the dissipated life he had formerly lived. Soon he ceased even to dine in his own home.

Some months went by in the enjoyment of this new independence; he was determined to preserve it, and in order to do so he separated himself from his wife, giving her the large apartments and lodging himself in the entresol. By the end of the year Diard and Juana only saw each other in the morning at breakfast.

Like all gamblers, he had his alternations of loss and gain. Not wishing to cut into the capital of his fortune, he felt the necessity of withdrawing from his wife the management of their income; and the day came when he took from her all she had hitherto freely disposed of for the household benefit, giving her instead a monthly stipend. The conversation they had on this subject was the last of their married intercourse. The silence that fell between them was a true divorce; Juana comprehended that from henceforth she was only a mother, and she was glad, not seeking for the causes of this evil. For such an event is a great evil. Children are conjointly one with husband and wife in the home, and the life of her husband could not be a source of grief and injury to Juana only.

As for Diard, now emancipated, he speedily grew accustomed to win and lose enormous sums. A fine player and a heavy player, he soon became celebrated for his style of playing. The social consideration he had been unable to win under the Empire, he acquired under the Resto-

ration by the rolling of his gold on the green cloth and by his talent for
all games that were in vogue. Ambassadors, bankers, persons with new-
ly-acquired large fortunes, and all those men who, having sucked life to
the dregs, turn to gambling for its feverish joys, admired Diard at their
clubs,--seldom in their own houses,--and they all gambled with him.
He became the fashion. Two or three times during the winter he gave
a fete as a matter of social pride in return for the civilities he received.
At such times Juana once more caught a glimpse of the world of balls,
festivities, luxury, and lights; but for her it was a sort of tax imposed
upon the comfort of her solitude. She, the queen of these solemnities,
appeared like a being fallen from some other planet. Her simplicity,
which nothing had corrupted, her beautiful virginity of soul, which
her peaceful life restored to her, her beauty and her true modesty, won
her sincere homage. But observing how few women ever entered her
salons, she came to understand that though her husband was following,
without communicating its nature to her, a new line of conduct, he had
gained nothing actually in the world's esteem.

Diard was not always lucky; far from it. In three years he had dissipated three fourths of his fortune, but his passion for play gave him
the energy to continue it. He was intimate with a number of men, more
particularly with the roues of the Bourse, men who, since the revolution, have set up the principle that robbery done on a large scale is only
a *smirch* to the reputation,--transferring thus to financial matters the
loose principles of love in the eighteenth century. Diard now became a
sort of business man, and concerned himself in several of those affairs
which are called *shady* in the slang of the law-courts. He practised the
decent thievery by which so many men, cleverly masked, or hidden
in the recesses of the political world, make their fortunes,--thievery
which, if done in the streets by the light of an oil lamp, would see a

poor devil to the galleys, but, under gilded ceilings and by the light of candelabra, is sanctioned. Diard brought up, monopolized, and sold sugars; he sold offices; he had the glory of inventing the "man of straw" for lucrative posts which it was necessary to keep in his own hands for a short time; he bought votes, receiving, on one occasion, so much per cent on the purchase of fifteen parliamentary votes which all passed on one division from the benches of the Left to the benches of the Right. Such actions are no longer crimes or thefts,--they are called governing, developing industry, becoming a financial power. Diard was placed by public opinion on the bench of infamy where many an able man was already seated. On that bench is the aristocracy of evil. It is the upper Chamber of scoundrels of high life. Diard was, therefore, not a mere commonplace gambler who is seen to be a blackguard, and ends by begging. That style of gambler is no longer seen in society of a certain topographical height. In these days bold scoundrels die brilliantly in the chariot of vice with the trappings of luxury. Diard, at least, did not buy his remorse at a low price; he made himself one of these privileged men. Having studied the machinery of government and learned all the secrets and the passions of the men in power, he was able to maintain himself in the fiery furnace into which he had sprung.

Madame Diard knew nothing of her husband's infernal life. Glad of his abandonment, she felt no curiosity about him, and all her hours were occupied. She devoted what money she had to the education of her children, wishing to make men of them, and giving them straight-forward reasons, without, however, taking the bloom from their young imaginations. Through them alone came her interests and her emotions; consequently, she suffered no longer from her blemished life. Her children were to her what they are to many mothers for a long period of time,--a sort of renewal of their own existence. Diard was now an

accidental circumstance, not a participator in her life, and since he had
ceased to be the father and the head of the family, Juana felt bound to
him by no tie other than that imposed by conventional laws. Nevertheless, she brought up her children to the highest respect for paternal
authority, however imaginary it was for them. In this she was greatly
seconded by her husband's continual absence. If he had been much in
the home Diard would have neutralized his wife's efforts. The boys had
too much intelligence and shrewdness not to have judged their father;
and to judge a father is moral parricide.

In the long run, however, Juana's indifference to her husband wore
itself away; it even changed to a species of fear. She understood at last
how the conduct of a father might long weigh on the future of her
children, and her motherly solicitude brought her many, though in-
complete, revelations of the truth. From day to day the dread of some
unknown but inevitable evil in the shadow of which she lived became
more and more keen and terrible. Therefore, during the rare moments
when Diard and Juana met she would cast upon his hollow face, wan
from nights of gambling and furrowed by emotions, a piercing look, the
penetration of which made Diard shudder. At such times the assumed
gaiety of her husband alarmed Juana more than his gloomiest expres-
sions of anxiety when, by chance, he forgot that assumption of joy. Diard feared his wife as a criminal fears the executioner. In him, Juana
saw her children's shame; and in her Diard dreaded a calm vengeance,
the judgment of that serene brow, an arm raised, a weapon ready.

After fifteen years of marriage Diard found himself without resources. He owed three hundred thousand francs and he could scarcely
muster one hundred thousand. The house, his only visible possession,
was mortgaged to its fullest selling value. A few days more, and the
sort of prestige with which opulence had invested him would vanish.

Not a hand would be offered, not a purse would be open to him. Unless some favorable event occurred he would fall into a slough of contempt, deeper perhaps than he deserved, precisely because he had mounted to a height he could not maintain. At this juncture he happened to hear that a number of strangers of distinction, diplomats and others, were assembled at the watering-places in the Pyrenees, where they gambled for enormous sums, and were doubtless well supplied with money.

He determined to go at once to the Pyrenees; but he would not leave his wife in Paris, lest some importunate creditor might reveal to her the secret of his horrible position. He therefore took her and the two children with him, refusing to allow her to take the tutor and scarcely permitting her to take a maid. His tone was curt and imperious; he seemed to have recovered some energy. This sudden journey, the cause of which escaped her penetration, alarmed Juana secretly. Her husband made it gaily. Obliged to occupy the same carriage, he showed himself day by day more attentive to the children and more amiable to their mother. Nevertheless, each day brought Juana dark presentiments, the presentiments of mothers who tremble without apparent reason, but who are seldom mistaken when they tremble thus. For them the veil of the future seems thinner than for others.

At Bordeaux, Diard hired in a quiet street a quiet little house, neatly furnished, and in it he established his wife. The house was at the corner of two streets, and had a garden. Joined to the neighboring house on one side only, it was open to view and accessible on the other three sides. Diard paid the rent in advance, and left Juana barely enough money for the necessary expenses of three months, a sum not exceeding a thousand francs. Madame Diard made no observation on this unusual meanness. When her husband told her that he was going to the watering-places and that she would stay at Bordeaux, Juana offered no difficulty, and at once formed a plan to teach the children Spanish and Italian, and to make them read the two masterpieces of the two languages. She was glad to lead a retired life, simply and naturally economical. To spare herself the troubles of material life, she arranged with a "traiteur" the day after Diard's departure to send in their meals. Her maid then sufficed for the service of the house, and she thus found herself without money, but her wants all provided for until her husband's return. Her pleasures consisted in taking walks with the children. She was then thirty-three years old. Her beauty, greatly developed, was in all its lustre. Therefore as soon as she appeared, much talk was made in Bordeaux about the beautiful Spanish stranger. At the first advances made to her Juana ceased to walk abroad, and confined herself wholly to her own large garden.

Diard at first made a fortune at the baths. In two months he won three hundred thousand dollars, but it never occurred to him to send any money to his wife; he kept it all, expecting to make some great stroke of fortune on a vast stake. Towards the end of the second month the Marquis de Montefiore appeared at the same baths. The marquis was at this time celebrated for his wealth, his handsome face, his fortunate marriage with an Englishwoman, and more especially for his love of play. Diard, his former companion, encountered him, and desired to add his spoils to those of others. A gambler with four hundred thousand francs in hand is always in a position to do as he pleases. Diard, confident in his luck, renewed acquaintance with Montefiore. The latter received him very coldly, but nevertheless they played together, and Diard lost every penny that he possessed, and more.

"My dear Montefiore," said the ex-quartermaster, after making a tour of the salon, "I owe you a hundred thousand francs; but my money is in Bordeaux, where I have left my wife."

Diard had the money in bank-bills in his pocket; but with the self-possession and rapid bird's-eye view of a man accustomed to catch at all resources, he still hoped to recover himself by some one of the endless caprices of play. Montefiore had already mentioned his intention of visiting Bordeaux. Had he paid his debt on the spot, Diard would have been left without the power to take his revenge; a revenge at cards often exceeds the amount of all preceding losses. But these burning expectations depended on the marquis's reply.

"Wait, my dear fellow," said Montefiore, "and we will go together to Bordeaux. In all conscience, I am rich enough to-day not to wish to take the money of an old comrade."

Three days later Diard and Montefiore were in Bordeaux at a gambling table. Diard, having won enough to pay his hundred thousand francs, went on until he had lost two hundred thousand more on his word. He was gay as a man who swam in gold. Eleven o'clock sounded; the night was superb. Montefiore may have felt, like Diard, a desire to breathe the open air and recover from such emotions in a walk. The latter proposed to the marquis to come home with him to take a cup of tea and get his money.

"But Madame Diard?" said Montefiore.

"Bah!" exclaimed the husband.

They went down-stairs; but before taking his hat Diard entered the dining-room of the establishment and asked for a glass of water. While it was being brought, he walked up and down the room, and was able, without being noticed, to pick up one of those small sharp-pointed steel knives with pearl handles which are used for cutting fruit at dessert.

"Where do you live?" said Montefiore, in the courtyard, "for I want to send a carriage there to fetch me."

Diard told him the exact address.

"You see," said Montefiore, in a low voice, taking Diard's arm, "that as long as I am with you I have nothing to fear; but if I came home alone and a scoundrel were to follow me, I should be profitable to kill."

"Have you much with you?"

"No, not much," said the wary Italian, "only my winnings. But they would make a pretty fortune for a beggar and turn him into an honest man for the rest of his life."

Diard led the marquis along a lonely street where he remembered to have seen a house, the door of which was at the end of an avenue of trees with high and gloomy walls on either side of it. When they reached this spot he coolly invited the marquis to precede him; but as if the latter understood him he preferred to keep at his side. Then, no sooner were they fairly in the avenue, then Diard, with the agility of a tiger, tripped up the marquis with a kick behind the knees, and putting a foot on his neck stabbed him again and again to the heart till the blade of the knife broke in it. Then he searched Montefiore's pockets, took his wallet, money, everything. But though he had taken the Italian unawares, and had done the deed with lucid mind and the quickness of a pickpocket, Montefiore had time to cry "Murder! Help!" in a shrill and piercing voice which was fit to rouse every sleeper in the neighborhood. His last sighs were given in those horrible shrieks.

Diard was not aware that at the moment when they entered the avenue a crowd just issuing from a theatre was passing at the upper end of the street. The cries of the dying man reached them, though Diard did his best to stifle the noise by setting his foot firmly on Montefiore's neck. The crowd began to run towards the avenue, the high walls of which appeared to echo back the cries, directing them to the very spot where the crime was committed. The sound of their coming steps seemed to beat on Diard's brain. But not losing his head as yet, the murderer left the avenue and came boldly into the street, walking very gently, like a spectator who sees the inutility of trying to give help. He even turned round once or twice to judge of the distance between himself and the crowd, and he saw them rushing up the avenue, with the exception of one man, who, with a natural sense of caution, began to watch Diard.

"There he is! there he is!" cried the people, who had entered the avenue as soon as they saw Montefiore stretched out near the door of the empty house.

As soon as that clamor rose, Diard, feeling himself well in the advance, began to run or rather to fly, with the vigor of a lion and the bounds of a deer. At the other end of the street he saw, or fancied he saw, a mass of persons, and he dashed down a cross street to avoid them. But already every window was open, and heads were thrust forth right and left, while from every door came shouts and gleams of light. Diard kept on, going straight before him, through the lights and the noise; and his legs were so actively agile that he soon left the tumult behind him, though without being able to escape some eyes which took in the extent of his course more rapidly than he could cover it. Inhabitants, soldiers, gendarmes, every one, seemed afoot in the twinkling of an eye. Some men awoke the commissaries of police, others stayed by the body to guard it. The pursuit kept on in the direction of the fugitive, who dragged it after him like the flame of a conflagration.

Diard, as he ran, had all the sensations of a dream when he heard a whole city howling, running, panting after him. Nevertheless, he kept his ideas and his presence of mind. Presently he reached the wall of the garden of his house. The place was perfectly silent, and he thought he had foiled his pursuers, though a distant murmur of the tumult came to his ears like the roaring of the sea. He dipped some water from a brook and drank it. Then, observing a pile of stones on the road, he hid his treasure in it; obeying one of those vague thoughts which come to criminals at a moment when the faculty to judge their actions under all bearings deserts them, and they think to establish their innocence by want of proof of their guilt.

That done, he endeavored to assume a placid countenance; he even tried to smile as he rapped softly on the door of his house, hoping that no one saw him. He raised his eyes, and through the outer blinds of one window came a gleam of light from his wife's room. Then, in the midst of his trouble, visions of her gentle life, spent with her children, beat upon his brain with the force of a hammer. The maid opened the door, which Diard hastily closed behind him with a kick. For a moment he breathed freely; then, noticing that he was bathed in perspiration, he sent the servant back to Juana and stayed in the darkness of the passage, where he wiped his face with his handkerchief and put his clothes in order, like a dandy about to pay a visit to a pretty woman. After that he walked into a track of the moonlight to examine his hands. A quiver of joy passed over him as he saw that no blood stains were on them; the hemorrhage from his victim's body was no doubt inward.

But all this took time. When at last he mounted the stairs to Juana's room he was calm and collected, and able to reflect on his position, which resolved itself into two ideas: to leave the house, and get to the wharves. He did not *think* these ideas, he *saw* them written in fiery letters on the darkness. Once at the wharves he could hide all day, return at night for his treasure, then conceal himself, like a rat, in the hold of some vessel and escape without any one suspecting his whereabouts. But to do all this, money, gold, was his first necessity,--and he did not possess one penny.

The maid brought a light to show him up.

"Felicie," he said, "don't you hear a noise in the street, shouts, cries?

Go and see what it means, and come and tell me."

His wife, in her white dressing-gown, was sitting at a table, reading aloud to Francisque and Juan from a Spanish Cervantes, while the boys followed her pronunciation of the words from the text. They all three stopped and looked at Diard, who stood in the doorway with his hands in his pockets; overcome, perhaps, by finding himself in this calm scene, so softly lighted, so beautiful with the faces of his wife and children. It was a living picture of the Virgin between her son and John.

"Juana, I have something to say to you."

"What has happened?" she asked, instantly perceiving from the livid paleness of her husband that the misfortune she had daily expected was upon them.

"Oh, nothing; but I want to speak to you--to you, alone."

And he glanced at his sons.

"My dears, go to your room, and go to bed," said Juana; "say your prayers without me."

The boys left the room in silence, with the incurious obedience of well-trained children.

"My dear Juana," said Diard, in a coaxing voice, "I left you with very little money, and I regret it now. Listen to me; since I relieved you of the care of our income by giving you an allowance, have you not, like other women, laid something by?"

"No," replied Juana, "I have nothing. In making that allowance you did not reckon the costs of the children's education. I don't say that to reproach you, my friend, only to explain my want of money. All that you gave me went to pay masters and--"

"Enough!" cried Diard, violently. "Thunder of heaven! every instant is precious! Where are your jewels?"

"You know very well I have never worn any."

"Then there's not a sou to be had here!" cried Diard, frantically.

"Why do you shout in that way?" she asked.

"Juana," he replied, "I have killed a man."

Juana sprang to the door of her children's room and closed it; then she returned.

"Your sons must hear nothing," she said. "With whom have you fought?"

"Montefiore," he replied.

"Ah!" she said with a sigh, "the only man you had the right to kill."

"There were many reasons why he should die by my hand. But I can't lose time--Money, money! for God's sake, money! I may be pursued. We did not fight. I--I killed him."

"Killed him!" she cried, "how?"

"Why, as one kills anything. He stole my whole fortune and I took it back, that's all. Juana, now that everything is quiet you must go down to that heap of stones--you know the heap by the garden wall--and get that money, since you haven't any in the house."

"The money that you stole?" said Juana.

"What does that matter to you? Have you any money to give me? I tell you I must get away. They are on my traces."

"Who?"

"The people, the police."

Juana left the room, but returned immediately.

"Here," she said, holding out to him at arm's length a jewel, "that is Dona Lagounia's cross. There are four rubies in it, of great value, I have been told. Take it and go--go!"

"Felicie hasn't come back," he cried, with a sudden thought. "Can she have been arrested?"

Juana laid the cross on the table, and sprang to the windows that looked on the street. There she saw, in the moonlight, a file of soldiers posting themselves in deepest silence along the wall of the house. She turned, affecting to be calm, and said to her husband:--

"You have not a minute to lose; you must escape through the garden. Here is the key of the little gate."

As a precaution she turned to the other windows, looking on the garden. In the shadow of the trees she saw the gleam of the silver lace on the hats of a body of gendarmes; and she heard the distant mutterings of a crowd of persons whom sentinels were holding back at the end of the streets up which curiosity had drawn them. Diard had, in truth, been seen to enter his house by persons at their windows, and on their information and that of the frightened maid-servant, who was arrested, the troops and the people had blocked the two streets which led to the house. A dozen gendarmes, returning from the theatre, had climbed the walls of the garden, and guarded all exit in that direction.

"Monsieur," said Juana, "you cannot escape. The whole town is here."

Diard ran from window to window with the useless activity of a captive bird striking against the panes to escape. Juana stood silent and thoughtful.

"Juana, dear Juana, help me! give me, for pity's sake, some advice."

"Yes," said Juana, "I will; and I will save you."

"Ah! you are always my good angel."

Juana left the room and returned immediately, holding out to Diard, with averted head, one of his own pistols. Diard did not take it. Juana heard the entrance of the soldiers into the courtyard, where they laid down the body of the murdered man to confront the assassin with the sight of it. She turned round and saw Diard white and livid. The man was nearly fainting, and tried to sit down.

"Your children implore you," she said, putting the pistol beneath his hand.

"But--my good Juana, my little Juana, do you think--Juana! is it so pressing?--I want to kiss you."

The gendarmes were mounting the staircase. Juana grasped the pistol, aimed it at Diard, holding him, in spite of his cries, by the throat; then she blew his brains out and flung the weapon on the ground.

At that instant the door was opened violently. The public prosecutor, followed by an examining judge, a doctor, a sheriff, and a posse of gendarmes, all the representatives, in short, of human justice, entered the room.

"What do you want?" asked Juana.

"Is that Monsieur Diard?" said the prosecutor, pointing to the dead body bent double on the floor.

"Yes, monsieur."

"Your gown is covered with blood, madame."

"Do you not see why?" replied Juana.

She went to the little table and sat down, taking up the volume of Cervantes; she was pale, with a nervous agitation which she nevertheless controlled, keeping it wholly inward.

"Leave the room," said the prosecutor to the gendarmes.

Then he signed to the examining judge and the doctor to remain.

"Madame, under the circumstances, we can only congratulate you on the death of your husband," he said. "At least he has died as a soldier should, whatever crime his passions may have led him to commit. His act renders negatory that of justice. But however we may desire to spare you at such a moment, the law requires that we should make an exact report of all violent deaths. You will permit us to do our duty?"

"May I go and change my dress?" she asked, laying down the volume.

"Yes, madame; but you must bring it back to us. The doctor may need it."

"It would be too painful for madame to see me operate," said the doctor, understanding the suspicions of the prosecutor. "Messieurs," he added, "I hope you will allow her to remain in the next room."

The magistrates approved the request of the merciful physician, and Felicie was permitted to attend her mistress. The judge and the prosecutor talked together in a low voice. Officers of the law are very unfortunate in being forced to suspect all, and to imagine evil everywhere. By dint of supposing wicked intentions, and of comprehending them, in order to reach the truth hidden under so many contradictory actions, it is impossible that the exercise of their dreadful functions should not, in the long run, dry up at their source the generous emotions they are constrained to repress. If the sensibilities of the surgeon who probes into the mysteries of the human body end by growing callous, what becomes of those of the judge who is incessantly compelled to search the inner folds of the soul? Martyrs to their mission, magistrates are all their lives in mourning for their lost illusions; crime weighs no less heavily on them than on the criminal. An old man seated on the bench is venerable, but a young judge makes a thoughtful person shudder. The examining judge in this case was young, and he felt obliged to say to the public prosecutor,--

"Do you think that woman was her husband's accomplice? Ought we to take her into custody? Is it best to question her?"

The prosecutor replied, with a careless shrug of his shoulders,--

"Montefiore and Diard were two well-known scoundrels. The maid evidently knew nothing of the crime. Better let the thing rest there."

The doctor performed the autopsy, and dictated his report to the sheriff. Suddenly he stopped, and hastily entered the next room.

"Madame--" he said.

Juana, who had removed her bloody gown, came towards him.

"It was you," he whispered, stooping to her ear, "who killed your husband."

"Yes, monsieur," she replied.

The doctor returned and continued his dictation as follows,--

"And, from the above assemblage of facts, it appears evident that the said Diard killed himself voluntarily and by his own hand."

"Have you finished?" he said to the sheriff after a pause.

"Yes," replied the writer.

The doctor signed the report. Juana, who had followed him into the room, gave him one glance, repressing with difficulty the tears which for an instant rose into her eyes and moistened them.

"Messieurs," she said to the public prosecutor and the judge, "I am a stranger here, and a Spaniard. I am ignorant of the laws, and I know no one in Bordeaux. I ask of you one kindness: enable me to obtain a passport for Spain."

"One moment!" cried the examining judge. "Madame, what has become of the money stolen from the Marquis de Montefiore?"

"Monsieur Diard," she replied, "said something to me vaguely about a heap of stones, under which he must have hidden it."

"Where?"

"In the street."

The two magistrates looked at each other. Juana made a noble gesture and motioned to the doctor.

"Monsieur," she said in his ear, "can I be suspected of some infamous action? I! The pile of stones must be close to the wall of my garden. Go yourself, I implore you. Look, search, find that money."

The doctor went out, taking with him the examining judge, and together they found Montefiore's treasure.

Within two days Juana had sold her cross to pay the costs of a journey. On her way with her two children to take the diligence which would carry her to the frontiers of Spain, she heard herself being called in the street. Her dying mother was being carried to a hospital, and through the curtains of her litter she had seen her daughter. Juana made the bearers enter a porte-cochere that was near them, and there the last interview between the mother and the daughter took place. Though the two spoke to each other in a low voice, Juan heard these parting words,--

"Mother, die in peace; I have suffered for you all."

The Codes Of Hammurabi And Moses
W. W. Davies

QTY

The discovery of the Hammurabi Code is one of the greatest achievements of archaeology, and is of paramount interest, not only to the student of the Bible, but also to all those interested in ancient history...

Religion   **ISBN:** *1-59462-338-4*   Pages:132

MSRP $12.95

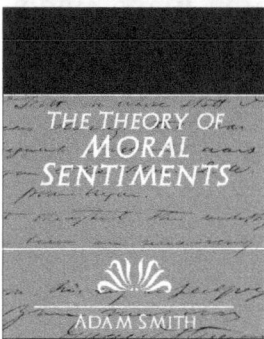

The Theory of Moral Sentiments
Adam Smith

QTY

This work from 1749. contains original theories of conscience amd moral judgment and it is the foundation for systemof morals.

Philosophy **ISBN:** *1-59462-777-0*   Pages:536

MSRP $19.95

Jessica's First Prayer
Hesba Stretton

QTY

In a screened and secluded corner of one of the many railway-bridges which span the streets of London there could be seen a few years ago, from five o'clock every morning until half past eight, a tidily set-out coffee-stall, consisting of a trestle and board, upon which stood two large tin cans, with a small fire of charcoal burning under each so as to keep the coffee boiling during the early hours of the morning when the work-people were thronging into the city on their way to their daily toil...

Pages:84

Childrens   **ISBN:** *1-59462-373-2*   *MSRP $9.95*

My Life and Work
Henry Ford

QTY

Henry Ford revolutionized the world with his implementation of mass production for the Model T automobile. Gain valuable business insight into his life and work with his own auto-biography... "We have only started on our development of our country we have not as yet, with all our talk of wonderful progress, done more than scratch the surface. The progress has been wonderful enough but..."

Pages:300

Biographies/   **ISBN:** *1-59462-198-5*   *MSRP $21.95*

The Art of Cross-Examination
Francis Wellman

QTY

I presume it is the experience of every author, after his first book is published upon an important subject, to be almost overwhelmed with a wealth of ideas and illustrations which could readily have been included in his book, and which to his own mind, at least, seem to make a second edition inevitable. Such certainly was the case with me; and when the first edition had reached its sixth impression in five months, I rejoiced to learn that it seemed to my publishers that the book had met with a sufficiently favorable reception to justify a second and considerably enlarged edition. ..

Reference   ISBN: *1-59462-647-2*

Pages:412

MSRP $19.95

On the Duty of Civil Disobedience
Henry David Thoreau

QTY

Thoreau wrote his famous essay, On the Duty of Civil Disobedience, as a protest against an unjust but popular war and the immoral but popular institution of slave-owning. He did more than write—he declined to pay his taxes, and was hauled off to gaol in consequence. Who can say how much this refusal of his hastened the end of the war and of slavery ?

Law   ISBN: *1-59462-747-9*

Pages:48

MSRP $7.45

Dream Psychology Psychoanalysis for Beginners
Sigmund Freud

QTY

Sigmund Freud, born Sigismund Schlomo Freud (May 6, 1856 - September 23, 1939), was a Jewish-Austrian neurologist and psychiatrist who co-founded the psychoanalytic school of psychology. Freud is best known for his theories of the unconscious mind, especially involving the mechanism of repression; his redefinition of sexual desire as mobile and directed towards a wide variety of objects; and his therapeutic techniques, especially his understanding of transference in the therapeutic relationship and the presumed value of dreams as sources of insight into unconscious desires.

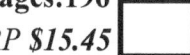

Psychology   ISBN: *1-59462-905-6*

Pages:196

MSRP $15.45

The Miracle of Right Thought
Orison Swett Marden

QTY

Believe with all of your heart that you will do what you were made to do. When the mind has once formed the habit of holding cheerful, happy, prosperous pictures, it will not be easy to form the opposite habit. It does not matter how improbable or how far away this realization may see, or how dark the prospects may be, if we visualize them as best we can, as vividly as possible, hold tenaciously to them and vigorously struggle to attain them, they will gradually become actualized, realized in the life. But a desire, a longing without endeavor, a yearning abandoned or held indifferently will vanish without realization.

Pages:360

Self Help   ISBN: *1-59462-644-8*

MSRP $25.45

QTY

The Rosicrucian Cosmo-Conception Mystic Christianity *by Max Heindel* ISBN: *1-59462-188-8* **$38.95**
The Rosicrucian Cosmo-conception is not dogmatic, neither does it appeal to any other authority than the reason of the student. It is: not controversial, but is: sent forth in the, hope that it may help to clear... New Age/Religion Pages 646

Abandonment To Divine Providence *by Jean-Pierre de Caussade* ISBN: *1-59462-228-0* **$25.95**
"The Rev. Jean Pierre de Caussade was one of the most remarkable spiritual writers of the Society of Jesus in France in the 18th Century. His death took place at Toulouse in 1751. His works have gone through many editions and have been republished... Inspirational/Religion Pages 400

Mental Chemistry *by Charles Haanel* ISBN: *1-59462-192-6* **$23.95**
Mental Chemistry allows the change of material conditions by combining and appropriately utilizing the power of the mind. Much like applied chemistry creates something new and unique out of careful combinations of chemicals the mastery of mental chemistry... New Age Pages 354

The Letters of Robert Browning and Elizabeth Barret Barrett 1845-1846 vol II ISBN: *1-59462-193-4* **$35.95**
by Robert Browning and Elizabeth Barrett Biographies Pages 596

Gleanings In Genesis (volume I) *by Arthur W. Pink* ISBN: *1-59462-130-6* **$27.45**
Appropriately has Genesis been termed "the seed plot of the Bible" for in it we have, in germ form, almost all of the great doctrines which are afterwards fully developed in the books of Scripture which follow... Religion/Inspirational Pages 420

The Master Key *by L. W. de Laurence* ISBN: *1-59462-001-6* **$30.95**
In no branch of human knowledge has there been a more lively increase of the spirit of research during the past few years than in the study of Psychology, Concentration and Mental Discipline. The requests for authentic lessons in Thought Control, Mental Discipline and... New Age/Business Pages 422

The Lesser Key Of Solomon Goetia *by L. W. de Laurence* ISBN: *1-59462-092-X* **$9.95**
This translation of the first book of the "Lernegton" which is now for the first time made accessible to students of Talismanic Magic was done, after careful collation and edition, from numerous Ancient Manuscripts in Hebrew, Latin, and French... New Age/Occult Pages 92

Rubaiyat Of Omar Khayyam *by Edward Fitzgerald* ISBN: *1-59462-332-5* **$13.95**
Edward Fitzgerald, whom the world has already learned, in spite of his own efforts to remain within the shadow of anonymity, to look upon as one of the rarest poets of the century, was born at Bredfield, in Suffolk, on the 31st of March, 1809. He was the third son of John Purcell... Music Pages 172

Ancient Law *by Henry Maine* ISBN: *1-59462-128-4* **$29.95**
The chief object of the following pages is to indicate some of the earliest ideas of mankind, as they are reflected in Ancient Law, and to point out the relation of those ideas to modern thought. Religion/History Pages 452

Far-Away Stories *by William J. Locke* ISBN: *1-59462-129-2* **$19.45**
"Good wine needs no bush, but a collection of mixed vintages does. And this book is just such a collection. Some of the stories I do not want to remain buried for ever in the museum files of dead magazine-numbers an author's not unpardonable vanity..." Fiction Pages 272

Life of David Crockett *by David Crockett* ISBN: *1-59462-250-7* **$27.45**
"Colonel David Crockett was one of the most remarkable men of the times in which he lived. Born in humble life, but gifted with a strong will, an indomitable courage, and unremitting perseverance... Biographies/New Age Pages 424

Lip-Reading *by Edward Nitchie* ISBN: *1-59462-206-X* **$25.95**
Edward B. Nitchie, founder of the New York School for the Hard of Hearing, now the Nitchie School of Lip-Reading, Inc, wrote "LIP-READING Principles and Practice". The development and perfecting of this meritorious work on lip-reading was an undertaking... How-to Pages 400

A Handbook of Suggestive Therapeutics, Applied Hypnotism, Psychic Science ISBN: *1-59462-214-0* **$24.95**
by Henry Munro Health/New Age/Health/Self-help Pages 376

A Doll's House: and Two Other Plays *by Henrik Ibsen* ISBN: *1-59462-112-8* **$19.95**
Henrik Ibsen created this classic when in revolutionary 1848 Rome. Introducing some striking concepts in playwriting for the realist genre, this play has been studied the world over. Fiction/Classics/Plays 308

The Light of Asia *by sir Edwin Arnold* ISBN: *1-59462-204-3* **$13.95**
In this poetic masterpiece, Edwin Arnold describes the life and teachings of Buddha. The man who was to become known as Buddha to the world was born as Prince Gautama of India but he rejected the worldly riches and abandoned the reigns of power when... Religion/History/Biographies Pages 170

The Complete Works of Guy de Maupassant *by Guy de Maupassant* ISBN: *1-59462-157-8* **$16.95**
"For days and days, nights and nights, I had dreamed of that first kiss which was to consecrate our engagement, and I knew not on what spot I should put my lips..." Fiction/Classics Pages 240

The Art of Cross-Examination *by Francis L. Wellman* ISBN: *1-59462-309-0* **$26.95**
Written by a renowned trial lawyer, Wellman imparts his experience and uses case studies to explain how to use psychology to extract desired information through questioning. How-to/Science/Reference Pages 408

Answered or Unanswered? *by Louisa Vaughan* ISBN: *1-59462-248-5* **$10.95**
Miracles of Faith in China Religion Pages 112

The Edinburgh Lectures on Mental Science (1909) *by Thomas* ISBN: *1-59462-008-3* **$11.95**
This book contains the substance of a course of lectures recently given by the writer in the Queen Street Hail, Edinburgh. Its purpose is to indicate the Natural Principles governing the relation between Mental Action and Material Conditions... New Age/Psychology Pages 148

Ayesha *by H. Rider Haggard* ISBN: *1-59462-301-5* **$24.95**
Verily and indeed it is the unexpected that happens! Probably if there was one person upon the earth from whom the Editor of this, and of a certain previous history, did not expect to hear again... Classics Pages 380

Ayala's Angel *by Anthony Trollope* ISBN: *1-59462-352-X* **$29.95**
The two girls were both pretty, but Lucy who was twenty-one who supposed to be simple and comparatively unattractive, whereas Ayala was credited, as her Bombwhat romantic name might show, with poetic charm and a taste for romance. Ayala when her father died was nineteen... Fiction Pages 484

The American Commonwealth *by James Bryce* ISBN: *1-59462-286-8* **$34.45**
An interpretation of American democratic political theory. It examines political mechanics and society from the perspective of Scotsman James Bryce Politics Pages 572

Stories of the Pilgrims *by Margaret P. Pumphrey* ISBN: *1-59462-116-0* **$17.95**
This book explores pilgrims religious oppression in England as well as their escape to Holland and eventual crossing to America on the Mayflower, and their early days in New England... History Pages 268

QTY

The Fasting Cure *by Sinclair Upton*   ISBN: *1-59462-222-1*   **$13.95**
In the Cosmopolitan Magazine for May, 1910, and in the Contemporary Review (London) for April, 1910, I published an article dealing with my experi-
ences in fasting. I have written a great many magazine articles, but never one which attracted so much attention...   New Age/Self Help/Health Pages 164

Hebrew Astrology *by Sepharial*   ISBN: *1-59462-308-2*   **$13.45**
In these days of advanced thinking it is a matter of common observation that we have left many of the old landmarks behind and that we are now pressing
forward to greater heights and to a wider horizon than that which represented the mind-content of our progenitors...   Astrology Pages 144

Thought Vibration or The Law of Attraction in the Thought World   ISBN: *1-59462-127-6*   **$12.95**

by William Walker Atkinson   *Psychology/Religion Pages 144*

Optimism *by Helen Keller*   ISBN: *1-59462-108-X*   **$15.95**
Helen Keller was blind, deaf, and mute since 19 months old, yet famously learned how to overcome these handicaps, communicate with the world, and
spread her lectures promoting optimism. An inspiring read for everyone...   Biographies/Inspirational Pages 84

Sara Crewe *by Frances Burnett*   ISBN: *1-59462-360-0*   **$9.45**
In the first place, Miss Minchin lived in London. Her home was a large, dull, tall one, in a large, dull square, where all the houses were alike, and all the
sparrows were alike, and where all the door-knockers made the same heavy sound...   Childrens/Classic Pages 88

The Autobiography of Benjamin Franklin *by Benjamin Franklin*   ISBN: *1-59462-135-7*   **$24.95**
The Autobiography of Benjamin Franklin has probably been more extensively read than any other American historical work, and no other book of its kind
has had such ups and downs of fortune. Franklin lived for many years in England, where he was agent...   Biographies/History Pages 332

Name	
Email	
Telephone	
Address	
City, State ZIP	

☐ **Credit Card**   ☐ **Check / Money Order**

Credit Card Number	
Expiration Date	
Signature	

Please Mail to: Book Jungle
PO Box 2226
Champaign, IL 61825
or Fax to: 630-214-0564

ORDERING INFORMATION

web: *www.bookjungle.com*
email: *sales@bookjungle.com*
fax: *630-214-0564*
mail: *Book Jungle PO Box 2226 Champaign, IL 61825*
or PayPal *to sales@bookjungle.com*

Please contact us for bulk discounts

DIRECT-ORDER TERMS

**20% Discount if You Order
Two or More Books**
Free Domestic Shipping!
Accepted: Master Card, Visa,
Discover, American Express